Angel on the Ward

James Edgar Skye

I dedicate this book to my mother, who changed the trajectory of my life in her passing in December of 2019. I know she wanted this story to happen, and so it became a reality.
I love you, and I miss you always.

Contents

Preface

This story is the work of fiction. In no way do I as the writer advocate self-harm or suicide. As the writer of this story, I come from this world and have lived through three suicide attempt, one suicide plan, and suicidal ideations. While this is a work of fiction, the ideas set forth by me, the author, are based on the reality of the mental illness world. I personally have spent time in psychiatric wards and what I write here does not reflect my every experience in these places or the actual experience of others. It is good look at a place where we lock up people without really understanding the consequences.

This story is a cautionary tale of what happens when we, as a society, let mental health go by the wayside. I wrote this story about the things I saw in my time in a psychiatric ward mixed with my own life experiences while taking a fictional creative approach to tell a story. The characters in what you are about to read do not reflect anyone in real life.

Suicide and self-harm are a part of living with a mental illness, and I believe that people who have never had to live that darkness can learn something within the words of this story. If the mental illness community is going to fight for better mental health, we have to show the realities of this world—and suicide is one of those realities. At the same time, fictional writing is one way of exploring the world of mental health.

J.E. Skye

www.jamesedgarskye.me
www.thebipolarwriter.blog
www.twitter.com/JamesEdgarSkye
www.patreon.com/jamesedgarskye
www.facebook.com/JamesEdgarSkye

Part One

JAMES AWOKE WITH a start as the opening of the overly large brown door that granted entrance into his room. With its slow opening it brought light into darkness. His eyes were immediately drawn to the light as the morning nurse's head became visible through a small head sized crack in the door. The nurse sought to see if he was still sleeping. Pausing for a moment to let her eyes adjust to darkness, James' eyes met her own, and she found her voice.

"When you're ready James, there's breakfast out in the common room," the nurse said. "You should try and get up, it's cold outside so dress warm."

James' greeting to the nurse was silence. Letting go of the door it slowly shut closed on its own, and the light from the hallway disappeared leaving James to the silence of the dark room.

With much chagrin, he sat up in his bed taking in his surroundings. With his hands be began to feel his body. First gripping the muscles of his arms and then feeling his calf muscles. His whole body was on fire and every bone hurt. If he could understand getting hit by a truck, this was the feeling he would imagine.

There was some bruising on his arms, and it took him some time to figure out where he now found himself. Frustration at his lack of recall, James gave up momentarily letting his head hit the pillow once again.

The last night was a blur at best. It was the worst experience of his life. His mind was being careful, it was easier to suppress the events of the night before rather than let the emotional pain consume his soul. This was folly of course, and as he lay in bed staring at the ceiling, his thoughts began racing around his head. Eventually the pieces of the night before began to flood back into his mind. Red hot tears began streaking down his cheek as the shame of remembering the night before became overwhelming.

" —shit," he said out loud to the open room. James knew that at there was nothing he could do but let the memories come into focus.

The truth was James could only remember the beginning and some the end of the previous night. The whirlwind of his memories was a haze. It was hard to distinguish what had been real and what were fake memories that his mind was using to suppress the truth. It was possible in James' mind that this reality he found himself in was fake and that right now he was at home in his bed sleeping.

The night before was as clear as the ocean, with the night sky full with the stars and the light of the moon reflecting back. After months of living in his dark thoughts, he finally made the decision that eluded his for so long — the decision to take his life. James wanted nothing more than to remove himself from this existence. James was ready to leave this Earth. His plan was to take all of his medication, which was mostly made up of sleeping pills, and he had finally worked up the courage. For weeks James poured over websites learning all he could about the best ways to end his life. His life was nothing of late as he was living with his parents and life was not what he thought it would end up growing up at twenty-two. While others were travelling and going to school he was lost in the throes of depressive thoughts and suicidal tendencies.

It was impossible to find a weapon and kill himself in that way. He read that there were people in the underbelly of society that sold firearms no questions asked, but as member of suburbia America, it was impossible that anyone he knew could get him a weapon — and worse he had no money to his name. He thought about cutting on his wrists with a knife, a novel idea, but he had no idea how deep he would have to cut, and if bleeding out was painless.

There was the option of hanging himself from the big oak tree next to his house, but that place had too many happy memories. It was just weeks prior that he was thinking of hanging himself from that very tree, but he lost his nerve when he realized that in every hanging in the movies he had ever seen looked painful—he wanted to path of least resistance.

That left him with two options. Walk down the street to the highway sit into oncoming traffic or take his medication. James wanted to die, but he wanted to not impact anyone else like a driver who was doing nothing wrong and would have to live with the guilt of his death or worse causing the death of another. James wanted no one to feel guilty about his death. A sentiment that he knew nothing about because at some level, James knew that no matter what he did this would be impossible. Someone would have to live with the guilt, and it would be his family. This was far from his mind, however, when the suicide attempt went down. Where he now found himself there was the feeling of regret that the night before had not gone as planned, not that he had tried to take his life.

He finally found himself staring down at the pills laid out on the table in front of him. The world around him had begun to go silent. A calmness came over James and every bad thought that he had over the last three months began to egg him on. The quietness was not unlike where James now found himself, in a plain room that was like a prison.

To stop the continuing flood of memories, James sat up again in his twin bed rubbing his fingers over his temple. A small sliver of light from the curtains was all he needed to take stock of his surroundings. The room was simple. It was small considering that two twin size beds took up most of the room, with two small nightstands made of mostly particle board. The cheap stuff that costs little to make. There were the two ugly brown cabinets, one directly in front of each bed pushing the limits of the small square room. The bed next to him was empty which James could appreciate given his circumstance. A smaller opening, smaller than the one the nurse had peaked her head in earlier was in between the cabinets. It had no door. A small bathroom from what he could see.

Lying around was getting his nowhere, and so he got up throwing the white hospital blankets to the floor. The short walk left a breeze in the back of his hospital gown. Illuminating the dark space, he realized the plainness of the bathroom was just as plain as the main room. James could only think he was in prison. It was not far from the truth—he was in the local psychiatric ward of the county hospital. His bathroom was similar to what you would find in a prison, a toilet, sink, and mirror. It was as plain as it gets.

The young man looking back in the mirror was different than the James of just three months prior. This version had sunken bloodshot deep-set jet-black piercing eyes. Around these eyes were the blackest of circles clashing against his light brown skin. The face staring back at him was lost, hopeless, and afraid. James was still wearing the hospital gown that someone had dressed him into the night before in the emergency room. His look became one of disgust and his thoughts of the emergency room began a new flood of memories.

James was semiconscious remembering very little from the moment he popped the sleeping medication into his mouth and how he was transported to the emergency room. Still there were things that came into focus as he continued to allow the thoughts to overcome his mind. He could still taste the black charcoal like substance that the nurses had shoved down his throat the previous night. It was the worse experience in his life, and he had no idea what the stuff was, but the after taste was horrid. The truth was so much more happened to James that night.

What he had failed to remember was the panic that his overdose suicide attempt had on his family. It was not by luck that his attempt to take his life was thwarted. When he decided to take his life, he said his goodbyes on social media alerting all that knew him that something was wrong. His parents found him in his makeshift room in their living room on the couch unconscious. They rushed him to the emergency room opting not to call an ambulance. It was a feeble attempt and it was not until years later that James would admit that this suicide attempt was a cry for help.

The sleeping medication made his memories fuzzy at best, but he remembered finally waking up just before he left the emergency room.

"We're taking him to the psychiatric ward, the doctors are holding him on a fifty-one fifty," a nurse said to James mother.

He woke up to the sounds of whispers just outside the drawn plain pink hospital curtain. A nurse was explaining the next steps to his mother. He could see the silhouette of the two and it was annoying that they were speaking in hushed voices. It was clear the talk was about him and he had no choice in what was happening next.

James remembered the long corridors and bright lights as a nurse and overweight security guard walked him to his new place of residence. The nurse was a small slight female, and she was wearing typical colorful nurse garments. If there was ever a different person than the nurse it was the security guard, who's heavy set frame made every step loud and pronounced. His heavy breathing was becoming increasingly louder as they walked side by side with James in a wheelchair. They whispered to one another to pass the time.

"What is this one going in for?" the security guard asked the nurse. They had no idea that James was listening, and he was curious as what the nurse had to say.

"Suicide attempt. I didn't get many of the details but when he came into the emergency room, he was unconscious and being dragged by his brother and father,' she responded.

"I will never understand how someone can do that to themselves," he said back.

The pair went silent as they came to stop in front of a large double door. James watched through the slits of his eyes the security guard press his badge against the reader on the wall. The large doors opened to reveal another long corridor. The pair continued their journey and their conversation with James listening.

"Do they normally do transfers of patients to the ward so late at night?" he asked.

"It depends. You must be new. Is it your first time making the long walk to the ward?"

"It's my second day. I'm not a fan of the graveyard shift," he responded, "but this is the second time I did a transport. My supervisor was with me earlier in the evening with a different nurse."

"It's common for suicide attempts to come in late at night. It's not the rule, but it happens more on the graveyard shift than any other, something about the late night that gets to these kids," she said.

"He's just a kid. It's crazy that these kids have nothing to live for, I will never understand it," he said.

James closed his eyes again as the bright lights illuminating the corridor began to hurt his eyes. It was a while before the nurse and the guard stopped again, this time at a thick and heavily locked brown door. An entrance to a whole new world.

"This is it," said the nurse. At this James opened one eye. He marveled at the sight in front of him. For the final time the guard pressed his badge to the reader on the wall with his right hand and with his left he opened the door. The wheelchair moved James and the nurse went forward, but the guard stayed behind. James heard the door close behind him.

The silence was deafening as the nurse made her way down to the nurse's station. James was still in a daze partly because of the drugs that made it into his system and from sheer exhaustion. What he did know was that something big was happening, but just how big he did not yet understand.

A small porky female nurse wearing plain pink scrubs made her way out of the nurse's station. She was much older than the other nurse, and James could see the wisdom in her eyes. The sight of an unconscious patient was nothing new for her. She placed herself in the path of the nurse pushing James' wheelchair.

"This must be James," the new nurse greeted the pair, "they said you were coming from the ER."

"This is him." The nurses began to talk amongst themselves for a moment leaving James a chance to finally open his eyes to his surroundings.

He could see the moonlight coming in from large set of glass windows in front of him. The room was very open and though parts of the room were in darkness there was enough light in the corridor that he could see couches and tables littering the open room. It seemed to James to be a common room of some kind, but not one he had seen before.

It was a while before the nurses finished their conversation and once again James was on the move. He closed his eyes again feeling the whole weight of the exhaustion that he was feeling. The trip was a short one and before long the nurses made their way with James through a door and into a room—the one James now found himself in.

James was impressed as both nurses helped him into bed while he partly pretended to be out if it. The porky nurse put the covers over him gently as the other made her way out of the room. The nurse turned out the lights closing the door behind her. It was the first time that James was alone, and the darkness overtook him. The tears streaking down his cheek were hot as he began to cry, and before long sleep overtook him.

He took one longer look at the face staring back at him before making his way out of the bathroom to the light switch in the room. With a flip of a light switch plastered to the wall, it made it easier for him to survey the room again. James noticed for the first time the paper bag on the nightstand and made his way the short distance. When he opened it a sense of relief washed over him.

From out of the bag he pulled out his favorite outfit. His pair of black skinny jeans, his Paramore T-shirt, and his black hoodie. For a moment James was confused and dumping the contents on the bed he noticed things were missing. He was sure that he had been wearing his shoes as he wanted to die in his favorite shirt, hoodie, and shoe combination—his all black Chuck's. It was one of the conditions that he made in his mind when he decided to end his life.

Panic began to overwhelm him, and he frantically made his way to the cabinet in front of his bed but all that faced him was empty shelves. All James could think was that this was very off. Why would they give him everything but his shoes?

With some annoyance at the start of his day, he put on his favorite outfit along with the fresh hospital socks and made his way out the door. It was much brighter now than when he made his way down the corridor the night before and he was taken aback when the open room came into view. James had never seen so much pink in his life. There were the pink couches up against the large glass windows. A small desk with a phone sat next to a glass door where a young pregnant woman was on the phone and yelling at someone in a pink chair. It was as if someone threw up Pepto-Bismol everywhere. The nurses were watching waiting to see if it would get out of control, but James thought that it was already there, but he decided it was not his problem. A glass door opened up into an enclosed atrium with a small forest from what he could see.

Beyond this area was a more open space with a plethora of tables and chairs with patients in the middle of breakfast. His feet moved in that direction and he found an empty table to sit down at, it was not long before a nurse came over to him with a tray of food.

"Here you go, dear," she said setting the tray in front of James.

He stayed silent preferring not to use words because he feared saying anything could mean something bad. James was slowly realizing the situation unfolding in front of his eyes. Everything from the last week, every horrible thought that crossed his mind, led him to this place. It was clear—he was trapped in this psych ward. He had heard of these places and used to laugh at people who ended up here, the irony now was burning into his mind.

James preferred to push around his food on his tray rather than attempt to eat. A habit that he picked up over the last few months. Slowly the people around him began to dissipate as they finished their breakfast. The place was loud, and the array of people were odd. It was a sight unlike anything he had ever encountered before. Some patients sat quietly intent on their own troubles, but there were a few were more rambunctious patients, and these people stood out the most to him.

His first thought was that what he was seeing was a dream, something out his worst nightmare. But James new this was a stupid thought and he pushed it out of his head deciding that these people were not worth the thought. As the young woman at the phone grew louder the nurse that gave James his tray made her way over to the girl.

"If you want to continue to use the phone, you're going to have to lower your voice, Jenna."

James could not take much more of the chaos and averted his eyes to his tray. He continued to push his food around. It was several minutes when something caught his attention. The door that he had come through the night before opened and a male nurse was pushing a young girl about James' age through the door in a wheelchair. Like the night before, the door closed behind them and the nurse wheeled the girl over to James' table.

James examined this girl with fascination. She was fragile, there was no denying it. The girl was skinny like she had skipped a few meals, though he could not see much of her arms. Both for her arms where heavily bandaged up from her wrists to where her elbows bend.

She tried to take away the pain, James thought to himself, and he could relate.

There were many nights that he thought about slitting his own wrists. He thought in retrospect maybe it would have been better than taking pills. Much like he had arrived the night before this girl was wearing a hospital gown with a white blanket in her lap. The nurse pushed her across the table from James and put a tray in front of her.

19

For a fleeting moment their eyes met, but like James she quickly looked down at her food afraid to make eye contact with anyone. He examined her closely through small glances in her direction. She was beautiful, there was no denying it even with the bandages. Her long black hair was matted but it only made her features like high cheekbones and hazel eyes more pronounced. Her skin was a light olive shade, and for a moment she raised her head. He felt embarrassed right away, but her hazel eyes penetrated his own stare.

He could not help himself, and he whispered so only she could here, "I'm James."

It was almost musical as she said, "Angel."

Part Two

LIFE MOVES QUICKLY on the ward, but for James it felt as if time was standing still. The first day for James was one surprise after another, and while he spent so much time alone lost in his thoughts, he could not shake Angel out of his mind.

James was not willing to concede anything and as he sat thinking about the past few weeks of his life. A new realization was dawning on him. James' only chance of getting out was to lie. He began to get his story straight in his head so that when he inevitably saw the doctor, he could tell them how he felt. It was to reconcile his truth with the actual reality of his plight. It was not easy for him to suppress more thoughts from becoming his present.

It was the darkest place James had ever found himself in, and it was all in his mind. For weeks leading up to the events of his last twenty-four hours was filled with turmoil. The emotional pain that James found himself the moment he opened his eyes each day was crushing emotional pain, and it hurt more than any deep cut.

Depression became his best and only real friend, and it was the only real thing in his life. His friend depression kept him up for days before he made the decision to take his life. The minutes ticked by stripping away any sanity that James was trying to hold on to until it became his everything. The reality in his mind was disorienting, and it was easy to let these dark thoughts start to take hold.

James knew he had no access to a firearm, and a large knife from the kitchen would not go unnoticed. Instead, he laid the remainder of his sleeping medication on the glass table and counted them out. He had almost two weeks' worth of pills and he believed that it would be enough to get the job done. For the first time in his life suicide and the taking of his life became real.

"James, it's visiting hour. Your mother and father are here to see you," said a nurse.

James was laying on one of the pink couches with the hood on of his favorite hoodie over his head shielding the light from his eyes. James moved to the farthest round empty table that he could find. A few minutes later his parents entered from a different door.

James' father was always a stern man. When he noticed James sitting at the table it was easy to see the anger in his father's eyes at the situation, he now found himself in. It was clear that his father was uncomfortable in this place. James mother was a different sight. James' mother always saw her son in the way that made her proud, but this was not a proud moment. He was always strong on the outside and her belief was that this was some kind of trick, James could see it in her eyes. There was no way her son could have done the things that now drew them to this uncomfortable situation. James mother wore a look of anxiety, sadness, and frustration.

James immediately became uncomfortable and the desire to flee was strong, but he wanted to get out of this place. If there were any two people that he believed could get him out now sat in front of him.

The three sat in silence each uncomfortable in their surroundings. James made the decision to break the ice, "What happened last night?"

James' dad spoke first, "You don't remember?"

"Not really. I remember I wanted to die, but that has passed. Obviously, I didn't really take my life otherwise I would not be here," he said.

Both his mother and father exchange a look before meeting his eyes again. For James, the need to want an end of his life was stronger than ever, but he was not going to let his parents in on this secret.

James continued the conversation as the pair were at a loss for words, "Am I getting out of here today? I mean it's not like I succeeded in killing myself. I don't belong here with these people."

"Son. They had to shove black charcoal stuff down your throat because of the sleeping medication you tried to overdose on," his mother said. Tears began welling up in her eyes. "You're lucky to be alive."

James could understand his mother's frustration. It was not even twenty-four hours since his suicide attempt. James could see that his mother wanted nothing more than for him to acknowledge that this was just a moment of weakness, but the truth would hurt her more. It was easier for James to placate and make his mother so she could feel good right now. He would deal with the consequences later.

His mother continued, "You're not getting out today, the emergency doctors put you on a seventy-two hour hold because of what you did."

"But, tomorrow is Thanksgiving. Are they going to leave me here? Are you—?"

"You put yourself here James," his dad said. His angry reply cut James off, "no one told you to take those pills. If you're stuck here it is only your fault, not ours. For weeks we have been on edge wondering if you would really try and take your life, you belong here forever if that's what it takes."

James could not meet his father's eyes. His father was right, but this was a defeat. He knew in his mind that this would be the worst possible scenario, and he was not going to give up. He would have to convince someone else. For the next forty-five minutes James and his parents went over details of the night before filling in James in on what had happened.

"We found you unconscious. Your best friend and your girlfriend called us after you said your goodbyes online. It took both of your brothers and your father to get you into the van. We thought about calling an ambulance, but we figured it would be quicker to take you ourselves to the emergency room," his mother explained.

"I wanted to just leave you be. You have already put us through so much over the last few weeks if you wanted to die, we should have just let you," his father added. James' mother gave her husband a look that stopped him in his tracks.

A nurse came up to the trio and said, "Visiting hours are almost over." The nurse walking away left the family to continue its conversation.

"I will be back later to visit. You need to call Victoria. She has been in hell since you were in the hospital. She is already on her way home from college," his mother said.

The pair got up and said their goodbyes. Watching his parents exit to the outside world was devastating for James and he felt envious. It was already an emotionally draining day, and it was not even lunch.

James made his way back to the common room which was mostly empty. The other patients on the ward were either finishing up their visits or in group therapy. The nurse had asked James if he wanted to participate in group, but he declined and instead did what his mother asked. This was one conversation he wanted desperately trying to avoid especially with another girl on his mind.

He knew however that it would be cruel to not let Victoria know that he was fine, with some reluctance reaching for the phone he punched the number to her cell number on the phone's keys. It only took two rings.

"Hello?"

"Hey, babe. It's me."

"Thank god. It's so good to hear you voice right now. I'm sorry," she said.

"Why are you sorry? You didn't try to take your life last night."

"I was not there for you. With everything that was happening I should have stayed home. Going back to school was a mistake—"

"Please don't do this again, Vic. I'm the reason why I'm here, not you," he said to her. He knew in his heart that Victoria was not the reason he now found himself in this place. James felt guilty at that moment that not once over the many long daily conversations with his girlfriend that he never once considered her feelings. James was a selfish, this he already knew, and it was wrong to keep hurting someone that wanted nothing more than to help him be happy.

"I'm on my way home. You mom told me that you're allowed visitors in the evening time. I should be home before that, and I will come and see you. I'll bring you your favorite Starbucks drink," Victoria said.

"Okay. I love you, Vic."

"I love you too, James."

James put the receiver back in its place and took the closest ugly pink couch laying down adrift in his thoughts about Victoria. It was so hard for him not to breakdown completely.

James had been with Victoria for over a year and despite the feeling of depression in every second of his day, she was the one bright spot in his daily life. From the moment that he saw her, James fell madly and deeply in love with her; it was always that way when he met a girl interested in him. It was hard to say what he liked more, her long black hair that

26

went down to the small of her back, her rounded prominent brown eyes, or the smile that brightened anyone's day. When Victoria looked at him in that way, with love, it made him smile. A rare thing for James.

She was out of his league and yet she was the first one to say "I love you" in the relationship. James wanted nothing more but to have her in his life. It started as a summer romance and for a fleeting moment James was happy, then as with most summer romances James and Victoria faced their toughest test—a long distance relationship as she had to go to school. It worked out for the first year of, but with James back at home and unable to work, his trips to Los Angeles where she went to school were becoming impossible. When they had another summer of beaches, backyard barbeques, and time cuddled on the couch, his life was good.

Victoria was worth the long-distance relationship in his mind and for the first few weeks of their second long-distance relationship James could convince himself that it would work out like before. But his depression was making his life hell and it became worse as the weather changed from the warm California weather in late October to the cold muggy November days. Those lonely nights began to take its toll. It was a confusing time for James because some weekends Victoria would make the drive up to visit him, or he would go and spend a weekend down with her. There were many happy moments between them. The moment that Victoria was not there, all he had was his old friend depression.

James was lost in these memories and time began to move a faster on the ward. It was not long before lunch was upon the patients. He made his way to what was becoming his favorite table—the furthest from anyone and empty. He had not noticed that the common room had filled while he was lost in his thoughts. It was a surprise to him to see Angel sitting at the same table they had shared breakfast. With more haste than before he made it to the table sitting opposite of her.

The pair began to eat their lunch in silence. James was struggling with the strange feeling in his stomach about a girl he knew nothing about and the girl he loved. It was becoming his obsession, was it a "brother and sister in arms" feeling? Or something more with Angel? James could not say. One thing was for sure, there was a real connection that he could not shake.

Angel was no longer in her wheelchair and James thought this was a good sign, but as she continued to eat in silence. He decided that it was not time to ask her questions. James was content to just sit and bask in her presence. A nurse broke the tension.

"James, the doctor is ready to see you if you're ready."

James nodded and pushed is tray away getting up from the table. He took one last look at Angel before following the nurse. The nurse took James down a short corridor that he had never been, and he watched as the nurse took him to a door that read "Psychiatric Ward Doctor."

The nurse knocked first before saying, "Wait here, the doctor will be with you in a moment."

After a few minutes the door opened to a young doctor who was looking at James through round spectacles that slightly came down his nose.

"Come in, James," he said. With his right hand he beckoned James to a chair facing a desk. The young doctor sat in the chair opposite James.

"How are you today James?" he asked. "You gave your family quite a scare last night."

James shifted in his chair uncomfortably, it was clear that he was not as ready to face the questions as he thought.

"I'm fine. I was really depressed last night. I had a temporary moment of weakness and I thought about ending my life. I might have tried to take too many sleeping pills, I don't really remember, and it's not like I succeeded," James said quickly.

He was proud of himself for a moment for thinking quickly. He knew that the only way to truly get out of this place was to make the doctor feel sorry about putting him here.

"I'm really sorry about causing everyone so much worry, it will not happen again."

The doctor looked down at his notes for a moment before speaking again, "This is not the first time that you have felt suicidal. In fact, your mother explained to the nurses last night that all this was going on for weeks now, since Halloween, maybe longer?"

James could feel the anger bubbling at the surface, it took all of him to say, "That was nothing really. Besides I saw a psych doctor and he prescribed be some sleep meds and an antidepressant. It just hasn't quite worked yet. I don't really like talking about this subject."

"And why is that?" the doctor asked.

It was harder this time and he had not intended the words to be so angry when he said, "It's because of you, the doctors. You never actually listen to me. I never wanted the medication to begin with but that is all you people seem to care about."

"Have you been taking your medication?"

"The sleeping ones, obviously."

"And the antidepressants?"

"I stopped taking them a week ago," James replied. "I hate how they make me feel worse. I'd rather just go without them."

The doctor began to write some notes on the pad in front of him before responding, "I understand that medications can be a hard adjustment. It't not a cure, but it can help you get better James. Your situation seems troublesome to me, were you hearing voices? I only ask because your mom mentioned it to the nurses last night."

This revelation made him pause for a moment. It was clear that this doctor knew more than what he previously thought. James knew he has to tread carefully before responding to this.

"Does it make a difference?"

"It does, James. Your diagnosis as it sits right now is schizoaffective disorder, it's a combination of schizophrenia and bipolar disorder," the doctor said.

"It must have been a side effect of taking the Ambien. It has been doing funny things to me. I would sleepwalk all the time. I once fell through a glass table while on this medication a few weeks back, my hoodie saved me from a lot of cuts and bruises. Did you ever think that everything that happened was a result of this drug?" James responded.

James knew this was false of course. The side effects of the Ambien were an issue, but it had nothing to do with his growing depression or the voices. He had only been on the sleep medication for about three weeks, and his depression and voices could be traced to perhaps years. James had been struggling for months with depression. The idea of depressive thought was something that he had some knowledge about, but these feelings were beginning to overwhelm him.

James had been working for a construction company as a purchaser. Before taking this job, he took a few months off after being let go as a seasonal painter. James was already showing the signs of someone in a deep depression mixed with mania. With the lack of knowledge at his disposal it became a push and pull in his life. The depression would make him not want to get up and go to work. When James was manic, he would spend frivolously running up his credit card debit and it began to take its toll on his mental health.

It was the only reason he took the construction job, was so that he had money to spend. For the six months he worked there his depression was not bad, but as all good things come to an end. The depression came back. One day he walked into his job and quit. There was no rhyme or reason. Over a year since, James was lost, and depression became his best friend and darkest companion. It made him feel taking his life was the only option. That was still true, but James wanted out of the psychiatric ward.

It was obvious that the doctor was not going to believe his tale. He responded with, "I want you to try something new. I know you're on Zoloft and I want to increase your dosage. I think a mood-stabilizer will also be helpful. Have you tried Lithium?"

"I have not."

"Let's try this over the next couple days and let us take you off Ambien for now. I will have the nurse administer your new medication later today," the doctor said.

James still had one question he desperately wanted to get out, "Is there any way that I can leave today? Tomorrow is Thanksgiving."

"I was hoping you would not bring it up. Sorry, the answer is no. You're on a seventy-two-hour hold, James. With the holidays you're going to be here until next week."

Part Three

JAMES LEFT THE OFFICE in a daze. Everything that could go wrong did, and a sense of frustration and defeat began to wash over him. His only thought was simple. If they were going to make him stay, he was going to make life on the ward impossible.

He made his way back to his room in no time laying down. He went over the discussion with the doctor in his head. James hated the idea that he had a mental illness diagnosis. In his junior year of high school, he took a psychology 101 class, and he knew all about mental illness, but his blood boiled at the thought he fit the bill. The people outside of his door, they belonged here.

The opening of the large door into his room broke his thoughts. A new nurse came in pushing a tray.

"James, I have your new medication that your doctor ordered," the nurse said. The nurse first opened a pill packet with pills with a blue diamond shape into a small paper cup—Zoloft his antidepressant pill. That he took it without question. The nurse handed him a small paper cup with water using it to swallow the medication.

The nurse then took a different packet from her tray and opening it she laid two oblong pink pills into the empty paper cup. James took the cup but looked at the pills.

"What is this?"

"It is your new medication, lithium," she said. "Your doctor ordered it."

"Do I have to take it?"

"Yes, James. You'll make your stay easier if you follow the program."

Reluctantly, James took the pills in his right hand also taking the water. With trepidation he puts the pink pills in his mouth with the water and swallowed them. The taste was like swallowing salt without water.

"Thank you, James," the nurse said, "There's a group therapy going on out there if you feel like joining."

"No thanks," he said coolly. Without a second glance the nurse made her way out of his room closing the door behind her.

James was not a fan of the idea of talking about his issues, to him he had none. Still, he knew that with many of the patients on the ward were in group therapy, the common room was open, and with that thought in mind he began the slow dreary walk to get out of his prison room. It was to his surprise to him when he saw that Angel was there sitting quietly on the couch. James stopped and thought about going back into his room, but at that moment their eyes met, he no choice he made his way to her.

"I thought the common room was empty," he said, "Can I sit?"

Angel gestured towards the seat next to her on the couch, and he took it.

In the quietest of voices that was quite angelic, Angel spoke her first sentence to James since they first met, "I know we met earlier. I'm Angel."

"James."

"I see you decided to skip group too," Angel said.

"Not great at sharing in any situation, so I made the decision to skip the talking about my feelings. The idea of sharing with people I don't know kind of makes me want to run away, only we are stuck here with nowhere to run," James said.

Angel's comforting smile made the two fell into a complementary silence. It was easy for James to be around Angel and not say anything. It was an unspoken bond that was becoming more defined as the pair stayed in proximity of one another.

Before long the nurses were calling out dinner was being served, and using the opportunity he said to Angel, "Can I sit with you and eat dinner?"

Her answering smile was all that he needed, and they made their way to the farthest of the dining tables, the one that was becoming a safe haven for the pair. Much like in the morning each ate very little of their dinner, and an unspoken communication began to crop up. When they would hear a patient yell uncontrollable profanity at the nursing staff, it only took a look between them to say, "I don't want to be with these people." With the culmination of dinner, a nurse came up to Angel.

"It is time you see the doctor, Angel," said the nurse.

Angel got up from her seat and the table pushing the chair in, and her goodbye wave made his heart leap. With much reservation James made his way back over to the ugly pink couches that had somehow become even more puke worthy and sat down next to the phone. It was the first time since coming to this place that James was around the other subjects of the ward, and he took this opportunity to take stock of his surroundings.

It was the most unusual group of people that he had ever seen. It was pretty even with male and female mentally sick people. There was one guy who did nothing but stare at the ceiling. *Did this guy ever blink?* It did not seem possible and yet the ceiling was a magical world that only he was able to see. There was the small group of three-woman patients gabbing away and in a circle on the floor. *This floor is tile, how is that comfortable?* He thought to himself. There was the young girl who was pregnant and at the same had the mouth of a sailor. *I never actually thought that Tourette syndrome was a real thing!*

It became clear that James felt out of place. Every single one of these people belonged here. It was a while before it became clear that he was being watched by another person on the ward. He had seen this group, the largest in the place, a few times since the morning. It was a gaggle of all-male patients, and when James eyes met the man that was watching him it became clear that he was their leader. A real feeling of high school hierarchy became apparent on the ward, and much like high school he was the odd man out.

James had never been one to be intimidated and when the realization that his guy was all about intimidation, he stared back making his intentions known. When the man, who was likely a couple years older than James, gave him a threatening look, his answer was a smile. That was all it took to make the leader walk over to James.

"Is something funny," he said to James. He came from where he was perched in the common area. This only made him want to smile more.

"Only that you seem to think this high school," James replied back. "Am I not allowed to look around or smile?"

"You can look wherever the hell you want, just not at me, is that clear."

James got to his feet before giving his response, "You don't scare me. You might outnumber me, but I think this," he motioned at the scene, "is just for show. Go bother someone else who can be intimidated."

This was all that was needed to change the group dynamic. Two, of what seemed like kids more James' age, began to flank the guy on both sides. He put his hand up stopping his friends as one of the male nurses began to approach on the group.

"Let him go. He's a nobody," he said. His posse began to back up, "Ryan, remember the name."

With that Ryan and his posse went back to their perch in the main part of the common room. James made his way to the outside to the atrium to get away from the noise. The atrium was a remarkable place. It was also a fake place. It was lush with green plants and trees that made the center of the atrium a magical jungle that made it seem that he was anywhere but a ward.

All around there were cement benches that, due to the time of year, they were cold to the touch when he sat down. He had to smile for two reasons: one, James was not one for confrontation, but he would never back down from a fight. Two, the atrium was not the worst place in the world. While it gave the illusion of peace, the fact that it was enclosed on three sides with cement walls, with the remaining wall all glass looking into the ward, only cemented the reality. *I am stuck in this prison.*

All James could do way lay down and look up at the cloudy sky above him, it was as peaceful as the place would allow. The passing of time on the ward can be a visceral experience but James could not help but think that time was slowing down again when he was not around Angel. At least the atrium was bearable without her.

He was laying down with his eyes closed for a long time before a nurse broke into his thoughts, "James, you have some guests waiting for you. Please make your way to the dining area."

When he made his way through the glass door, he saw his mother and his sister at a table, right in the middle of all the people visiting other patients.

"Hey bro, how are you doing? You gave us a scare last night," his older sister said. His mother sat next to her and she had been visibly crying. It was clear now that she was trying to exude that she was okay.

He tried to keep it light, "Sorry about that, it was just a temporary thing. It won't happen again, I promise."

This seemed to placate his family members at least in the interim. His sister continued, "We brought you some things that should help your time here feel more like home."

From the floor his sister took a large paper bag that was overflowing with items and she slid it across the table. With the bag in front of him he began to remove the contents to the table. From the top was more clothes that were similar to what he was wearing—all black without much color. The final count was three shirts and an extra pair of pants. *Still no shoes?* From there he took out several books from his mother's collection.

"We thought you could use some books," his mother said. "There is also your MP3 player charged up. They would not give you the headphones or charger directly. They said you could get them at the nursing station. You can only listen to it in the common room."

From the bag he found the remaining item—his iPod music player. A sense of relief began to wash over James. If he was going to be here for a while, at least he could have some items of comfort.

"Thank you, mom, and you too, sis. I talked to the doctor earlier. I'm here until next week at the earliest."

"I know," his mother responded back, "I talked to the doctor before I came here. Look I know it is not ideal, but this is the best place for you right now."

This annoyed him, "What does that mean?"

His mother gave a sheepish look, "Come on son. You knew something like this was possible. All the times in the past three weeks that you said that 'you wanted to die was leading you to this place."

James, who was already dreading the future, felt especially chastised by his mother's words, but after a moment he understood. *She is scared of what is happening and she thought this was the safest place.* At that moment a man, much too large to squeeze between James and the table chose to push his entire body against his chair pushing him towards the table. James chose to ignore this, but his sister tried her best to stifle a laugh with a cough.

"Can you not," he said quickly but in a quieter voice, "I have to live here."

"Sorry bro, but come on, that was funny."

The large man did not disappoint and a moment later he did the exact same thing going back to his table he came from with a cup of water in his hand and James once again had to squish himself into the table. The smile on the man's face only made his sister laugh harder. James gave her silencing look.

His mother changed the subject, "Victoria is out there waiting. We are going to take the first half hour and she will take the next."

"How is she?"

"She is hurt, James. She feels like this is all her fault. Be nice to her please, she is struggling with a lot and she is missing work. At least she is off school right now. I tried to tell her to stay in L.A., but she wanted to be here."

"I won't make it harder on her, I promise."

The remaining time that James had with his family moved rather quickly and before long they were making their way out into the outside world. After a few minutes, he could see Victoria making her way through the large door to the outside and to the table. He got up hugging her and pecking her on the lips before they both sat down. She brought with her a small token. James' favorite Starbucks drink, the one they had on their first date—an iced passion tea.

"How are you James?" she said. She put the drink down in front of him before taking the seat next to him.

"Okay. It has been kind of tough being in here," he said, "Look Vic, I'm sorry. I should have called you instead of taking those pills. I looked at your number for hours on my phone, but you have your life down there in L.A., and well my life is here. It isn't fair to you that—"

"Don't do that James. You know I love you more than anything in this world. Me going to school it was just something that I needed to do, but I can come back—"

"No, Vic. That's not what I meant. You have to continue your schooling, no matter what happens with me here," James said.

"Wait. What does—"

Realizing the phrasing of his little speech he cut Vic off, "I don't mean like I'm not going to be here. It is more like this place is where I belong for the foreseeable future."

"What did the doctors say?" she asked.

Not leaving out any details he explained to Victoria about his conversations with the doctor and how it was looking like he would miss Thanksgiving with his family. He could see the pain her hazel eyes and it made him regret the last twenty-four hours of his life. *I should have just called her and talked it out. Why are you such an idiot James?"*

"You know you don't have to be here," he said staring down at the table, "I would understand if you went back home. I know you were planning to stay down there for Thanksgiving and coming up here for Christmas."

"It's fine. My parents will be happy with me being home, and I think they would prefer it that way."

"Do they know?"

"I had to tell them why I was back. They understand, James," she said.

"I'm not worth the trouble Vic—"

"Don't James, "she said cutting him off. "I know you better than you think. The first sign of trouble and you want to bail. I'm not giving up on you."

James could see the love for him in her eyes. It was the same way for him, but he knew that deep down that he was in for more trouble in his future. *Could I really bring her along knowing that my future is so uncertain?*

"You know I love you right, Vic?" he said. It was with a twinge in his stomach that he reluctantly as he said this to Victoria as his mind began to wonder to Angel.

"I love you too, James. More than you know."

It was a trying evening for James, so much of his day was apologizing for something he felt he had done nothing wrong. It was easier to placate the ones that loved him than to share his real thoughts. Victoria got up to leave and James got up to follow her, but at the last minute with a pivot she threw her arms into James kissing him deeply. The washing guilt that overcame him was defeating. Victoria left the ward without another word.

Two opposites had taken over his mind. On the one side was Victoria, the love his life. On the other side was Angel, who was? *What was she to me? A familiar?* The point was moot as he made his way to the nurse's station with all of his belongings.

The nurse looking up from her computer, "What can I do for you, James?"

"My mom said that you allow me to listen to my music in the common room," he pulled the small iPod from the bag, "I have my player here and music for me is a calming type of therapy."

The nurse quietly spoke to the nurse next to her and she made her way to a row of small cubby holes. From the angle he could see "James" on one of the cubbies where the nurse pulled out his headphones. She made her way to the stations entrance opening it making him move back.

"There are some rules before I hand you these," she showed him the headphones and the long headphone jack that started at the top off the headphones and with the end reaching the ground. "These are dangerous here, so you can only use them in sight of the nurse's station. When you're done with them you must return them. Are you going to comply with these rules?"

With a glance first at the nurse and then to his headphones he made his decision, "That works for me."

Without a word the nurse hands the headphones over to James and he made his way to what was becoming his favorite ugly pink couch. He set the bag full of his belongings next to the couch and laying down he could see the large white tiles of the roof that had water damage. With his headphones on he put his favorite band, Paramore, it was easier to drown out the opposing thoughts about Victoria and Angel. James noticed once again that one of the nurses was making her rounds.

It can't be time for more medication, can it?

Watching the nurse make her rounds it was clear that she was heading his way and before long she was attempting to talk to James over the noise of the music.

"I need to take your blood pressure, James." she said. The nurse moved the machine close to James placing the cuff on his right arm. The blood pressure machine did its thing and after a few moments the nurse removed the cuff. James began to lay back down but the nurse with a motion told him that he was not done.

"Sorry James. I also have some medication for you—"

"What the hell? I already took medication this morning, why so I have to take more? The doctor stopped my sleeping medication, didn't he?" he asked in a raised voice.

"Your doctor prescribed lithium in the morning and late afternoon or evening. Please James, make this easy. I have a lot of rounds—"

"I refuse to take it." he said. James crossed his arms in defiance.

"You have two choices here: take the medication or face the consequences. Why not make it easy?"

"Screw this—" With a blur James grabbed all his belongings and ran past the nurse, past the common room, and down the short hall to his room. He could hear the quick footsteps of his pursuers and the cheers of the patients. Closing the door behind him he threw his things on the bed and sat down in a defensive position.

James could see the nurse just outside the room, but she was not coming inside. James found this a curious thing. He laid his MP3 player and headphones on the bed. He knew that whatever came next was not good, but he didn't want to lose this privilege. *I fucking hate this place*. Minutes began to pass, and the nurse only stood outside his room, but after a few more moments the reason became obvious.

The nurse that tried to administer his medication opened the door flanked by two male nurses and a security guard, the overweight one from the night before.

"Now James, this is not the behavior that is going to help you in the long run. Can you please take your medication?" she asked. In one hand she reached out the medication as an offering, but James knocked the medication out of her hand scattering the pink pills to the floor.

"That was not wise." She motioned to the male nurses to James' bed and with one on each side the pair raise James off the bed. At first, he was willing to take what was coming to him, but a rage began to overcome his rational side. First, he tried to shake the nurses, but they were considerably stronger than him, and they began to drag instead of leading him to the destination. This only made the anger rise inside him and a string of profanity with the aim at the nurses left his mouth.

As soon as it had begun, he was taken into a room with all white padding walls and a single door in and out. It reminded him of what you see in psych wards in the movies. The nurses laid him carefully on the floor and then walking out to the freedom outside this new prison within a prison.

Before the medication nurse left, she turned to face James. The other two nurses and the security guard crowded outside the door. "You will be in here until you calm down." Without another word she walked out closing the door behind her.

The rage and anger were strong with James and the continuance of profanity was worse than before. Kicking the door and pounding his fists did nothing. They could not hear him. After some time, he conceded defeat laying down on the floor. Red hot tears began to fall down his cheek, he had fallen so far in this life, and this was his rock bottom.

Part Four

JAMES WOKE THE NEXT morning in his bed. He had cried out his eyes and after an hour the nurses returned to the padded and apparently soundproof room to fetch him like a dog in trouble. Without a word he took the medication that the nurse offered him drowning it with the water—his throat hurt so much from the yelling that the water was a refreshing change. The nurses escorted him back to his room where he was left to his thoughts that once again began to consume his every second. It was very late, and it was not long before sleep overtook him closing his first day on the ward.

He sat up in his bed. It was still dark outside his single window and his room was still empty without a roommate. Next to his bed on the nightstand was two paper bags, one of which was the one his mother gave him the night before, the other from the nurses. Before returning him to his room they had taken his stuff off the bed putting it neatly on his bedside table.

James knew in that moment that the day before was the worst day of his life. *How could so much happen in one day?* He thought about what was happening and the loss of control he was now feeling. It was clear that the nurses were not taking any crap from him, and the night before was proof that he could hit the lowest level of his life and still find the rocky bottom. It was becoming clear to him that this psych ward could become a permanent situation because there was something seriously wrong, even if he was not ready to admit it.

He didn't know if these thoughts were good or bad. The belief in his mind since he came to this place was that he in this place was wrong. He was coming around to the idea that maybe his behavior was not helping him score any positive points in this place. If he was to leave this place forever there was room for his attitude to improve. James got up slowly to his feet and as they hit the cold floor, he moved to the window and could see a glimmer of the sun over the buildings adjacent to his room. The dawn brought a new realization—it was Thanksgiving Day.

It was still early, but James began to dress in fresh clothes, one of the nurses left two pairs of hospital socks on his nightstand. You know the ones that have strange bumpy things at the bottom that their only purpose is to keep you from falling down on the slippery floors. It was warmer with the socks on than off, so he reluctantly put them on. Rummaging through the brown paper bag he found a book to his liking and made his way out of his room to the common area of the ward.

The sun was barely peeking into the common area and it was completely empty as the occupants of the ward were still in their beds. James passed the nurses station without a word. He knew that an apology should be coming to the nurses, but the night before was still raw in his mind. He made his way to his favorite pink couch and began to read his book. While reading, the ward around James came to life as people began to move around the common room to start their day. He stuck to his book not wanting to make any waves. From the corner of his eyes occasionally he would scan the room in hopes of catching Angel making her way to the dining area.

When the morning nurse made her call on him for breakfast Angel was already sitting at the farthest table. She had come from the opposite side of the ward on the other side of the dining area. He could see a nurse bringing a tray to her, and he made his way through the breakfast crowd to her table sitting across from her. The nurse brought a tray to him and steam came out when it was open.

With a surprise, Angel was the one that started the conversation, "I hear you had a rough night." She smiled at him and for the first time that morning he thawed out.

"I wasn't my best last night. Actually, it was horrible the way that I acted," James said.

"It's this place. It does something to you if you let it. You have let this world come to you especially when you have never been here before," she smiled again. "Sorry. I could tell the first day we met."

"It's fine. I take it you have been here a few times?"

"It's not my first time," with that she began to rub her right arm, "it will probably not be the last. I'm a lifer, or that is what some of the patients and nursing staff call people like me."

"I'm sorry. That can't be easy. I have never self-harmed, but I have thought many times about slitting my wrists just to watch them bleed. I know it can be so easy to give into the physical pain to push the emotional pain away."

"Thanks. You know you're the first person to say that to me since I got here. My family pretty much gave up on me a long time ago and the nurses know me so well that they don't care. My parent's figure there is nothing they can do to stop me from harming myself. What about you, I don't see any marks, you're here for a similar but different reason?" she asked.

"Overdose on my sleeping pills. I wanted to sleep forever—" he stopped before finishing his sentence. It was unlike James to be so open. Since he was a kid, he always kept his emotions close to his chest. It was easier to pretend that everything was okay than to actually let himself feel things and be honest. He had no idea why he was so open to Angel since coming to the ward he had done nothing but lie.

"Well," she said, "Glad you're still here."

"Thanks," he said. For the first time in weeks he smiled. The pair finished their breakfast in silence. With their trays gone, they both made their way to the common room. It was a while before they picked the conversation back up, but when it did, the conversation was like wildfire.

It was easy to talk to her and he quickly found out that they both had so much in common. She was a fan of alternative rock and was into the same bands that he loved. They talked about Paramore, and James told her how over the summer he had gone to Warped Tour and saw them live with his girlfriend. He was able to be at the front of the stage and see Hayley Williams herself and she had slapped him high five—it was the highlight of his life outside of Victoria. She came up often in these first conversations.

Angel talked about how growing up she was always quiet about her likes and dislikes because her family was very strict and very religious. When she was younger, she wanted to be teacher and she excelled at math, but when her mental illness began to overtake her life as a teenager her dreams fell to the distant and unattainable.

"I have lost a lot in the past few years. I didn't walk with my high school class because I was here," she motioned to the surroundings, "hopefully this could be my last time, or that is something I always tell myself. It's hard to say. I tried to tell me my doctor that I want to get better, but he doesn't believe me. I don't blame him, most people in my life have given up on me."

"I can't imagine being in this place so many times, it has already been a tough time in the short time I have been here, and this is my first time."

"So, what are you reading," she asked.

"It's a murder mystery book. I know it sounds kind of morbid, but books like this pique my interest. The author is one of my favorites, she was once a forensic pathologist and she uses that experience in her novels," he said.

"You seem really passionate about your books," she said, "I prefer music over books. I love to listen to music. Did I tell you I used to play the guitar?"

"No. That's amazing. I could never play being a lefty it was always hard for me to pick it up. I do love to listen to music and guitar play. It helps me get through some of my dark thoughts."

"I know the feeling—"

At that moment a nurse came over interrupting the conversation, "It's almost time for visiting hours, James."

"Okay," the nurse walked away, and he turned to Angel, "Is anyone visiting you today? It's Thanksgiving after all."

"No visitors for me today," she said. With a small sigh, she got up from the couch and heading towards the girls dorms.

James did the same thing putting away his book. His room was on the opposite side of the ward. When he made his way back to the visiting area, he found his mother sitting at a table with a plate of food.

"Hey mom."

"Hello, son," she said.

"Do you want to go outside to the atrium? It is quieter out there," James said. His mother silently responded with a shake of her head yes, and he grabbed the plate of food making his way outside.

"You look better son. I couldn't get anyone to come here with me, but I brought you some Thanksgiving food," she said. "I couldn't sleep last night so I have been cooking since one this morning."

"Thanks mom. You didn't have to do that, but I'm hungry. I didn't really eat much breakfast, the food here sucks," he said.

He began to inhale his mother's cooking as he always did as she was the world's greatest chef. As he ate it made him sad when the realization that this would be his first Thanksgiving ever without his family, and more importantly he truly missed watching how happy cooking made her. It was something that he always took for granted, but with every bite the guilt about the last year of his life began to overwhelm him. How much he must be hurting his mother was making the guilt worse than ever.

It changed little in his mind though because he desperately wanted to not be a part of this world. To be or not to be, was all too real in James' life. But it was easy to placate his mother in the now and the rest of their visit he gave his mother hope that things would change. It was selfish, but he knew it was the only way.

"How's the family taking me being in here?"

"Your father is furious, and I doubt he will be visiting you the rest of the time you're in here. Your brother is back in town from school. He will probably visit with me sometime this week," his mother said.

"That's good to hear. Not surprised about dad. Tell him that I'm sorry about the trouble I have been causing. Let him know when I get out things will change," James said.

"James don't make promises that you can't keep. This has been going on for months, maybe longer," she paused for a long moment. "Why did you do it?"

James was not ready for this line of questioning. It was inevitable but he knew that the truth was far too damaging. He decided that his response will be only parts of the truth, and the rest will be what his mother desperately wanted to hear.

"It just happened mom. I was sitting there depressed and out of my mind. I honestly didn't mean to do it. I was missing Victoria, but I couldn't reach out to her. The sleeping pills were just there, and it was so easy to just take them and dream of not being here, I never thought it would kill me."

"And your goodbyes on social media?"

"It was just a cry for help, and now I can get help in here," he said.

That seemed to be enough for his mother in James' mind though he didn't know it at the time that his mother knew that it was not the whole truth. She wanted her son out of this place and back into her care where she believed that she could help him get back on track. If that meant that she had to placate him, then she was willing to do it.

With the visiting hours winding down James' mother got up to leave, but before she left there was one more thing on her mind.

"I was talking to Victoria last night. She feels like you're being distant with her. I like her, and you need to treat her better. Call her. She is coming by at the late visiting hours with more food. Make things right," she said. With that, his mother left the ward.

It was not like his mother to get in the middle of his relationship but given the fact that Victoria's visit the day before had not been great, it was not a surprise that they had talked. He knew at some level she was hurt because of what he said. He wanted Victoria to do nothing but live her life far from his madness. Victoria was the sweetest most beautiful girl that ever gave James the time of day. Vic was the best thing that ever happened in his life.

With the visiting hours over the common room began to fill with noise as people made their way towards group therapy that seemed to always happen after visiting hours.

50

James sat alone finishing his Thanksgiving meal waiting for the common room to be completely empty. When he was done, he took the paper plate with the small amount of remaining food and found a garbage can. He was desperate to hear Victoria's voice.

"Hey, James."

"How did you know it was me?" James said.

"I don't recognize the number, but it's our area code. I was waiting for your call."

"Sorry about yesterday. I was in a bad place."

"I get it babe," she said back.

"Last night was a rough night. I spent part of it in a quiet room." It was easier to tell her it was a quiet room than to explain that this room was a bad place for patients that failed to follow the rules of the ward.

"What happened?"

"I might have knocked the medication out of the hands of a nurse and caused a major scene," he explained. James had rarely shown Victoria the anger side because hiding it from her was easier. "Okay, I might have lost my temper it can get when things didn't go my way. I never like change. They're changing my medications and giving me new ones. I just want out of here for good."

"James you have to be willing to make the changes. I was researching last night, what did they give you that was new?"

James had always loved this about Victoria, she was a natural researcher and it was no surprise that the first thing she did was research everything that was going on in his life. It only made him love her more.

"They started me on lithium and raised my antidepressant."

"I thought they would start you on that. Look, babe, you have to take the medication as the doctors prescribed. I think it will be better for you."

"For you, I will."

"Good. I will be there for the next visiting hour. I told your mom I would pick up more food at the house before I leave for there."

"She told me. I will see you then my love."

He put the phone in its holder and his thoughts were even more confused. He loved Vic more than anything, but the more that he stayed on the ward, the closer Angel was a part of his orbit. He could not pinpoint what was going on.

The afternoon on the ward was very quiet for James as he kept to himself. He read his book outside in the atrium and though it was very cold he preferred the silence. It seemed that no one really used this place and it was the solitude that he liked. It has always been like that for most his life. Even in high school he had a set of friends, but most of the time it was easier to be alone and playing video games on the school's computers.

Playing video games was the one area in James' life that he had always excelled at since he was a young kid. The first memories of gaming were in elementary school and playing Pokémon on his Gameboy color. He was always proud of his gaming accomplishments, but it had also been the best escape from the depression. Since the day that he walked out of his job after quitting he had used video games as an escape. It was only when Victoria came into his life that he found that he had more reasons to leave the confines of his house.

The last year had been hard. To make money he worked part time with his uncle at his shop and he sold most of his DVD collection to make money. When that was not working, he would ask his mother for money. It had been like that for months, but James was struggling so much. It was not that he didn't want to work, in the times in his life work was a part of his life, and he was a hard worker.

His second job was proof of that he was a hard worker. At the time he was working through a temp agency and they had assigned him to unload trucks at a local plumbing and heating company. He showed that he was willing to work, even if it was just pushing a broom around the warehouse. He showed real initiative and the next week he was driving a truck route and putting in 1,500 miles on the road a week. Like most things in his life, this was only temporary, and he quit after eight months. It was a few months in unemployment before he found work again.

His next job was a summer apprenticeship at a painting company. It was only supposed to be seasonal, and he enjoyed his time at the company. At the end of the summer an incident with a foreman, he claimed that James was unwilling to help him load a power washer into the truck and he got hurt, it meant that he was laid off. It was not until the end of that year that he found his last job.

If James thought about it, there were so many signs that he was dealing with a mental illness. It could be denial, lack of knowledge about mental illness, or perhaps the stigma of mental illness that kept him from seeking help, but the signs were glaring. It finally came down to that fateful night not two days earlier that he made his life altering decision.

It had been sometime since James had seen Angel and he was getting worried that she was mad about the question about her visitors. If he had been truly paying attention, he would have realized that her relationship with her family was shaky at best.

James' afternoon was a quite affair and it was not until just before dinner time before he saw Angel again. First, he had to endure another visitor's time, and this time he had to be happy to see his girlfriend. It was Thanksgiving after all, and he could be thankful for Victoria in his life.

Victoria's visit was just what his mother wanted, he talked to her about how sorry he was about what he said the day before. They talked about what had led to the events that landed him in the isolation room and he apologized and chalked it up to his frustration at being stuck in the ward for the foreseeable future. The visit would have been better if it was just his girlfriend, but she brought her sister along with the food. Her sister was far from holding back judgment.

"Are things going to change when you get out of this place," her sister Spencer asked. "You know, Victoria deserves better than what you're putting her through right now."

James and Spencer had a love and hate relationship. She was two years older than James, but in a small town with two high schools they knew one another. Victoria was three years younger than James and Spencer would have preferred that her sister was single and dating while she was in college instead of a serious relationship. She made it known to James when they got together that their relationship was doomed because Victoria was heading to school in the fall. They both lived down in Southern California now, and Spencer had been trying to get Victoria to leave James since she started school.

"Like I told Vic, yes things are going to change. It has been a rough year for me, but this experience has taught me a lot about the right and wrong ways of going about my issues."

"Good," she responded. With that she left to wait in the lobby. James watched her with disbelief.

"Sorry babe, Spencer is just looking out for me. You do look better today. Did you take my advice?"

"Yes. I have been taking my medication when they give it to me and staying out of trouble. I want to get out of here as soon as possible—"

"And get better, right?" Victoria interrupted.

"Of course," he said. Deep down at some level James did want to get better if only for Victoria. He would do anything to make her happy.

"Good. Hey, I have to leave early today. My mom is waiting for me to get back home to start Thanksgiving dinner," she said. Victoria pushed the plate of food over to James. "Your mom made you a little of everything."

"It's fine. Go spend time with you family. I love you and tell your family everything is okay. I don't want your mom worrying about me."

Victoria got up and came over to James's side and embraced him. "I love you too, James. Please be safe in here and get out of this place. I hate seeing you like this."

She kissed James lightly on the lips and departed.

It was near dinner time on the ward, but James was not interested in eating the hospital food with the care package his mother had sent along. As he began to make his way out to the atrium, he saw Angel.

She smiled before saying, "That smells good."

"Would you like to join me? There is plenty of food for both of us. I can ask the nurse for an extra fork."

"You don't mind?" she asked.

"Of course not," he said, "Here take the food and I will ask for an extra fork at the nursing station."

James made the short walk to the nurse's station quickly but had to wait a moment for a nurse's attention.

"What can I help you with, James?"

"Can I have an extra fork, please? I wanted to share my Thanksgiving food with another patient," he said pausing for a moment. "Is that allowed?"

"Sure, it's fine. Where are you going to eat the food?"

"In the atrium."

"That is fine," the nurse said. Handing the plastic fork wrapped in plastic to James and he made his way back to the atrium. Angel was already sitting patiently on a bench that was obscured by the trees and plants. Sitting next to her and handing over the fork, she tore away the plastic and they quietly begin to eat James' Thanksgiving meal.

"Your mom is an amazing cook," she said, "You know you should tell her that more often. Your mother seems like a major part of your life, not all of us have that kind of support."

James felt bad at this, and Angel was not far off. James was not the best person over the last year. It never occurred to him that his actions hurt those around him. His mother, Victoria, friends, and family had all felt the wrath of his ongoing issues with mental illness. It hurt James still to say that it was because of his depression, because denial was an easier pill to swallow.

"I know. I just..." he stopped wondering if he should say the truth. He decided it was best, "I have been in this really dark place. An inner voice keeps a constant stream of my worst thoughts that I can't escape from."

"I know that inner voice well. It's the most significant part of depression, do these thoughts race through your mind?"

"All the time," he responded.

"You have to figure out what part of the darkness is true and what is it trying to take you deeper into the dark thoughts."

"Is there any way out?"

"I believe so," she responded, "at least for some. Not for me. There is hope in you, James, there is a light in you that I saw the first day we met. I think that you don't see it. You're special, and you have so much to give to this world. You will survive this, and it won't be forever."

The pair finished the plate of food and for a while they watched the grey pallet of the afternoon sky began to darken, they could both feel the heat that their bodies were creating sitting next to one another. It was special to both to sit together in silence and it was becoming the happy place by her side on the ward. After a while a nurse came out to check on the two and administer their medication.

"There's a movie going in the common room. We bring in a television and tonight the movie is *Breakfast at Tiffany's*," the nurse said. She was talking to James more than Angel. James assumed it was because they knew her so well.

"Do you want to come along?" he asked Angel. "I love that movie."

"I would love to." James took Angel by the hand leading her into the common room.

Part Five

JAMES WOKE THE NEXT morning with the strangest feeling in his stomach, it was somewhere between euphoria and disheartenment. The night before he had been the best night he had since coming to the ward. He watched his favorite movie with Angel sitting next to him holding his hand, and he had walked her to the women's side of the ward. The only thing James failed to do was to kiss her goodnight.

Then the disheartening part—Victoria. There was no doubt in his mind that she was the love of his life. From the moment they met, there was no one else. And yet, now there was someone else—Angel. This was turning out to be one of those confusing times you read in novels. He felt guilty. James held the hand of a woman that was not his girlfriend. But was it more than just someone that could be there for him while he was in this horrible place? Was she a shining light of beacon in a place that James would rather be anywhere else?

James did his best to justify that he had only wanted comfort and holding Angel's hand throughout the movie was just a momentary lapse of judgment. *Should I tell Victoria and hurt her?* Two things James was certain about, he absolutely loved Victoria, and there was a part of him, he didn't know how much, wanted Angel in his life.

It was maddening to James and with that he got up and started what was becoming his "ward" morning routine. It was not much of a routine, but the nurse from the night before had offered to send his clothes to the laundry to be washed. He found his clothes—his favorite hoodie, jeans, Paramore t-shirt, and a new pair of hospital socks—neatly folded in the cupboard in his room. In no time James was out of his room book in hand and making his way to the common room to read before breakfast.

It should have been a quiet morning, but as James would find out this day it would not start out so great. Ryan and his gaggle of mates were sitting in front of the television talking rambunctiously about the music video blaring on the television. It was a hip-hop vides where all the girls wore very little, which left little to the imagination. While James could understand the culture, it was not for him. James looked around hoping to find Angel, but she was nowhere to be found. James lingered a moment too long and before he could decide to walk back to his room Ryan's focus became James.

"Well if it isn't guy who gets visitors two times a day from family and a hot girlfriend, it must be nice," he said. Ryan decided to get up from the couch determined to get in James' way, his cronies followed like loyal little lap dogs. James could not help but feel the hurt by the meaning behind his words.

James wanted to let it go, he wanted desperately to stay out of trouble. The goal was to leave this place, but with the tugging of his heart between Victoria and Angel, his patience was thin.

"Yeah, I have people that love me, I can't say the same for you. What was your name again? Ryan? Who cares to remember, I haven't seen one person visit you—"

That did it. Before James could finish Ryan pounced with all intentions of swinging at James. He knew it was coming, and the fact that Ryan outweighed him by fifty pounds made it easy to duck and pushing his whole body into his adversary the momentum took both men to the floor where they scuffled for a bit. Ryan was clearly the stronger of the two, but James was scrappy and could hold his own. The blows were mostly to the body and by the time the male nurses separated the two neither had been hit the other in the face. By some miracle, or the fact that they could not believe that James actually fought back, Ryan's friends stayed out of the fray.

As the nurses separated the pair Ryan had time to say, "I'm going to get you. Just wait."

James could only laugh as the male nurse, holding his arm, began to move him towards the hallway where he has met his doctor earlier. The nurse knocked on the door motioning James to sit on one of the pair of chairs just outside the door. When the door to the psychiatrist's door opened James is surprised to see a different doctor than the one he saw before. *Great. This can't be a good thing.*

James patently listened to the nurse's play-by-play. Lucky for James the nurse was coming to his defense and with the mention of Ryan the doctor nodded with understanding. It was clear that Ryan had his own reputation here in the ward. As the nurse continued his conversation with the doctor, he realized that it was not all roses for himself, and he was starting to build a reputation of his own.

James did not notice right away that the doctor had an accent during the conversation with the nurse, but when he dismissed the nurse and motioned him into the office he could tell right away.

"Come in, James," he said, "I see you're not getting along with one of the other patients. Sit, please." James took the seat just opposite the doctor.

"I didn't start anything. I was going to the common room to read my book," he said. He realized at that moment that in the commotion he had dropped his book. "All I want to do is get out of this place, and yet you guys keep me here for no reason."

"Sorry you feel that way, but you're not here for nothing."

"Will you release me today?" James asked in earnest.

"It's not possible," he said, "I'm the only psychiatrist here to help out during the holiday weekend. The only one that can release you is the psychiatric ward doctor who is not here until Tuesday."

"Isn't that great—"

Before James could finish the door to the office swung open with a rush and a nurse stuck her head in.

"Doctor, we need you. One of the patients got a hold of something sharp in her room. The emergency personnel are already with her. They need you."

"Please stay here, James." He said. With that the doctor exited the office quickly with the nurse on his heels leaving just out of James' sight but with the door ajar. James wondered out loud who had found something sharp and tried to take their life. There was one person that he knew that could and would do something exactly like that, it was someone that just the night before he had spent his time holding her hand.

She would not do that, not after last night? he said to himself.

James began to think about the night before in a different context. Yesterday was Thanksgiving and no one came to see her. In fact, since the moment he met her, not one person had come to see her. What had she said the night before?

"Is there any way out?" he had asked her.

"I believe so," she responded, "at least for some. Not for me. There is hope in you, James, there is a light in you. I think that you don't see it. You're so special, and you have so much to give to this world. You will survive this, and it will not be forever."

Was she telling James goodbye? Was the holding of his hand her last chance at having someone be there one last time? It was so different for James. Angel was the connection to this place that was positive. She was the light in the darkness that was the psych ward. Now that James had thought about it, how was this place for Angel? *"You're so special, and you have so much to give to this world. You will survive this, and it will not be forever."*

Angel was trying to tell James and he failed to see the reality. That sharing his food showed her that some people have someone. That for James no matter what he did people loved him. It was different for Angel. She didn't want to be a part of this world just like him, but there would always be his mother or Victoria trying to save him. James had always thought that someone cares about everyone, but everyone had given up on Angel.

It was too much for James and he decided that he had to know for sure. He made his way down the hall to where the woman's part of the ward was, and there was a group of patients forming a crowd. Several nurses were keeping the patients back. James moved through the small crowd with ease, and noticed Angel was not among the crowd. James' heart began to race, he wanted to push forward and see.

"James you have to stay back, please," said the nurse.

"Who is it?"

The nurse only shook her head. The crowd began to dissipate as what was going on in the room just out of their sight began to bore the gathering patients. Before long it was only James that was standing there, and he was willing to wait out the event. He passed the time with pacing and lost in thoughts. Breakfast was being served but he wanted no part of it.

As breakfast finished James got his first glimpse as a gurney was being pushed by nurses trailed by the psychiatric doctor. Before long, his worse fears were realized, on the gurney was Angel, her left wrist heavily bandaged again. She caught his eye for a moment and then the group was gone through the doors of the psych ward. Would James ever see her again?

Part Six

LIFE BEGAN TO MOVE slowly. Angel had entered his life a beacon of light in this place that he hated more than anything. How could she do such a thing to herself? It did not take long to realize that he was being a hypocrite. It was not three days earlier that he attempted to take his life? James was being especially hard on her considering he still wanted to end his life, just not on the ward. Angel had been helping him through the process of dealing with the ward, and James had done nothing but be his usual selfish persona. Only caring about getting himself out of this place. Angel had reached out, James was sure about it now, and he did nothing.

That was James life over the last year. There was not one person that he thought about other than himself. Victoria had done nothing but believe in James and loved him despite his issues with mental illness. If anything, she loved him more and was always looking to understand. How many times throughout her day had she texted James that she loved him or to check on him? It was more than James had done. When he tried to take his life, he didn't say goodbye to her and never thought about what it would mean if she lost her boyfriend.

His thoughts moved to his family. For the last month James was a terror. From moment to moment they had no idea what James was a going to do. End his life? He threatened to do that weekly if not daily leading up to his suicide attempt. He never thought about how embarrassing it was for his family when he said goodbye to the world on social media for all to see. *How much had he hurt his mother and cared about nothing in this world but not being a part of it? No wonder my dad wants nothing to do with me.*

Since his arrival on the ward he had done nothing but complain about being in a place where he felt he did not belong. The truth was that James was a selfish person and could not see past it, but now seeing what Angel was capable even in this controlled environment changed everything.

James imagined his life as Angel. No Victoria telling him that she loves him with all her heart. A family that gave up on him and he lived in places for the mentally ill or even worse on the street. No one in his life to worry about him. No one to visit. James, trying again and again to take his life but this time without anyone to say, "Please stay." The depth of loneness that was Angel's hopelessness was something that frightened James beyond reason. It was a life with no one. James began to question if he ever really wanted to die.

With the confusion of the morning events, the visiting hours were pushed and the events between Ryan and James had gone by the wayside. James spent the last few hours laying on his bed thinking about everything. One idea was becoming very clear. Things had to change in his life, and it started with one thing.

James found himself outside the psychiatrist's office not realizing that his feet were taking him into that direction. He could tell the office was occupied only by the doctor and so he knocked on the door.

There was a quiet moment before the psychiatrist said, "Come in."

Opening the door, he sat opposite the doctor.

"James, sorry I was going to call you back, the events of this—"

"I didn't come to talk about that," he said. Then changing his mind, "Is Angel going to be okay?"

"I can't discuss another patient. If you're not here to talk about your events this morning, what is on your mind?"

"I want to ask a question first," said James.

"Ask."

"What is my official diagnosis?"

"Officially, schizoaffective disorder. The psychiatric ward doctor gave you that diagnosis in the hospital. Your mother mentioned that you hear voices from time to time. Do you?" he asked.

James wanted to ignore this, but it was time for honesty, "If I say I did, and those voices were telling me that I had to end it all, what does that mean if I no longer hear them?"

"I was under the impression that you told the other psychiatric doctor there was nothing wrong with you?"

"Maybe I have not been truthful," James said, "but I have changed my mind considering the events over this week. Maybe I believe that there is something seriously wrong with me."

"That is an amazing first step. Can I ask what brought this on?"

"Angel. I have gotten close to her and I see how much pain she is in. She told me she has no one in her life and that is a scary thing—to live this mental illness life with no one," James said. "I don't want to lose everyone in my life. I was in denial, but this place and seeing Angel continue to not want to be here, it scares me."

"This is big James. However, there is always the chance that you're just saying what we want to hear."

James was expecting this reaction, but unlike before, he was ready with the truth, "Then I will have to prove it to you. You say I have until Tuesday or later perhaps. It's only Friday. I will show you that I can accept my illness and the medication."

"Have you really stopped hearing voices?" the doctor asked.

"Not sure if it was hearing voices or just my inner dialogue, at the moment, no."

"I will write that down. This is a positive step. I would like you to join group therapy this afternoon. Is that something that you see yourself doing?"

"I can do that. I might not talk but it would not hurt to try."

The weekend would be the biggest test for James on the ward. While his resolve to finally admit that there was something wrong was stronger than ever, it was so much easier to let things he promised go by the wayside. Making his promise to go to group therapy was not attempted until Saturday. When he arrived and saw everyone sitting in a circle, James regretted the decision and chose not to participate and just sat in quiet contemplation.

His thoughts were of Angel and where she was, perhaps in some hospital room recovering. It was lonely on the ward without someone to talk to and it was showing with quiet frustration while James spent most of his free time with a book in hand drowning out the world. Since his visit with the psychiatric doctor on Friday, he was already on his third book by Saturday. There was some excitement however, and he was looking forward to one thing—visitations. Due to the incident with Ryan, the doctor had taken away his visits for the day before, and he had not had the chance to tell Victoria and his family that he was going to start changing for the better.

James' first opportunity came when Victoria visited him in the morning. When James saw her his heart began its quick pace that it always done when he saw her. Today her long jet-black hair that always went pass her back was in a tight bun and somehow her hazel eyes sparked when their eyes met. But it was her smile, the one he felt in that moment, he could never live without. Victoria's smile illuminated any room.

Embracing her tighter than usual Victoria he gave a passionate kiss to Victoria on the lips before he let her go, she looked around with some embarrassment at the other visitors. He could see the faint flush of red in her cheeks.

"You okay?" she asked.

"I'm good babe. I just miss you is all. No big."

Victoria smiled at this handing him his favorite Starbucks drink. He sipped as the pair sat next to one another. She put her hand in his.

"What happened yesterday that kept you from being able to have visitors?"

"Ah, there is this patient in here that doesn't like me or the fact that I get visitors all the time. We got into a tussle and I lost visitations. I should have walked away, but you know I have issues walking away."

Victoria knew all too well that James had a temper especially when he drank. Two months before they had been at a favorite haunt of James and his friends. Like usual, James was drinking and playing pool always for money. He was in a game with two others around his age and while they were playing one of the guys began to flirt innocently with Victoria. She had politely told him that she was with James, but this infuriated him, and it was not long before he was in the face the man ready to take on anyone. It was only Victoria that was able to get James to calm down and leave. Victoria now wondered if his mental illness had a lot to do with his anger.

"Are you passed all that, you're still here for a few more days," she asked. "I can tell things are changing in you."

"I'm over it. Not sure if he is," he stopped to look around and point towards Ryan. His back was to James as he watched the television. "I'll do my best to avoid him the rest of my time here. Anyway, that's not what I want to talk about."

He paused for a moment to gather his thoughts. This was a major step in his mental health, and he wanted to convey that he was telling the truth, and not just telling Victoria what she wanted to hear.

"I was talking to the doctor yesterday after all that happened, and I made a decision. One I hope that you will like, I admitted that there is something wrong with me."

Victoria was taken aback by this news. The last month all James would say when she would bring up the issue of having a mental illness was that she was wrong. That the doctors were wrong. That there was nothing wrong with him. He told her that so many times a day a small part of her believed him that was until he actually tried to take his life. It made her believe otherwise. But now he is admitting he did have a problem. Victoria wanted nothing more to be optimistic, but she was very cautious.

"You, James, told someone that there is something wrong with you. And you meant it?"

"Every word."

Victoria pinched herself on her arm in a very cliché way, "Nope, not dreaming. Maybe I just don't know I'm dreaming?"

"It's real Vic, I promise. Things in here, events with people has changed my perspective. Look I'm not "saved" or believe that the medications are a necessary thing for me to get better. I still believe that I can do it on my own, but I'm not an expert so I will take the medication to see if it helps," James explained.

"And have the medications worked?"

"Honestly, maybe. I feel different. Hey, my mom told the doctor that I was hearing voices, she told the emergency room nurse. I thought I was but is it true?" James asked.

"That is what you were yelling on the way to the hospital. You said the voices were telling you to take your life," she explained, "You don't remember anything about that night?"

"I remember bits and pieces and what my parents told me. Like laying my sleeping pills on my laptop keyboard in a neat pile and staring at them in the darkness for a really long time. I remember taking them and bits of pieces of before I got to this place. I just didn't know I actually said I hear voices."

"Have you since?" she asked.

"Nope," Victoria looked at him incredulously, "honest to God, in no way shape or form am I hearing voices."

"Okay," she said and paused. "What changed? You have been more than adamant about the fact that nothing was wrong with you."

James had to stop and think about his response to Victoria carefully. Since being in the psych ward, his love for her had not changed one bit. If anything, the fact that she came home and was visiting him daily had made James love her more, but she would not understand him getting close to another girl. To not hurt her, at least this what he told himself, he gave her an abbreviated version.

He began with the details, "I was in the doctor's office talking about the fighting incident when a nurse came in. Apparently, during the night one of the patients had tried to slit her wrists. She came up with something sharp. I heard the nurses say that they had no idea where she had the sharp object that she used. The whole thing kind of put my life into perspective."

By time James had finished telling the story Victoria was looking more worried than ever. She said with fright in her voice, "Tell me James that you will never do that, tell me this change is real and never again."

"I promise you with everything in my heart, Vic. Never again."

Part Seven

JAMES' VISIT WITH VICTORIA was a positive one and when it came to his visit with his mother in the evening, he told her that he was going to work on changing, but without the gruesome story of why he had changed his mind. His mother was more optimistic that Victoria, but it was because she was more scared of what the alternative of not getting better meant for James. She wanted nothing more than for him to start on the right path and get better right away.

James was quietly eating his diner at the farthest table from the rest of the patients lost in his book when the door that opened from the hospital flung open—it was Angel returning to the ward. The nurse that was pushing took her straight to her room. This bothered James a bit as he wanted desperately to have a conversation with her. He had to make amends for not realizing how much pain she really was in on Thanksgiving Day.

He was not allowed on the women's side of the ward, no male patient was, so in order to visit her, James had to get creative. It was far from easy. That evening when his plans to visit Angel in the night had formed in his mind, the ward decided that he was to have a roommate. This James thought would be an issue, but the man was mostly lethargic and by the time James plan started to become a reality his roommate was fast asleep.

James had been watching the nurses for the better part of an hour. His view of the nurse's station was the first obstacle that he would have to face. The upside was that at one in the morning only two nurses were at the station, but its position at the middle of the ward posed some issues. One nurse was there to roam and the other to watch for patients like James from leaving their rooms. It was a stroke of luck that one of the nurses left towards the door that led out of the ward. The other nurse began her rounds on the male side of the ward.

Seeing this, James hastily made his way to his bed. He could see through the slits in his eyes the nurse looking into his room before moving on. Back at the door, he could see the nurse looking in the adjoining room before leaving to turning the corner. It was the opportunity he was waiting for all night.

With the quietest movement he opened his door ajar just enough so that he could slip his skinny frame through the door, and with a bit of resistance from body up against the door it closed without a noise. Moving both quickly and cautiously he made his way to the nurse's station. A double check told him that it was indeed empty. With some haste now he walked through the common room, through the dining area and down the hall to Angel's room. Like the door to his room he opened it just enough to slip in. The light and closing of the door woke Angel with a start. He was lucky that she didn't have a roommate.

"James?" she said to the darkness.

"Yeah it's me," he said almost at a whisper. James made his way to the other side of the bed that was not easy to see from the door.

"What are you doing here?" she asked. He could see even in the darkness that Angel was crying. He didn't know how but he could tell it had nothing to do with the cutting of her arms. It was something else. Something all too familiar to James—emotional pain.

"I had to see you. I had to apologize—"

"Why would you have anything to apologize for? You did nothing. I—" she stopped trying to make the tears stop. "I'm damaged goods James, leave me alone. I can't help you. Hell, I can't help myself—"

The door to Angel's room opened slightly and James ducked down making his body into a ball on the floor. Angel turned not letting the nurse see that she was awake. Lingering for just a moment the nurse closed the door.

"Angel. I didn't realize that you were still in pain. I was selfish," he said while he was still down. He was trying his best to help Angel, but he was quickly running out of words to say. Their time was also limited. He figured that the nurses would be checking his own room again at some point in the next hour. James raised himself to the bed and wiped away her tears.

"Why did you do it, Angel? Why didn't you tell me what was going on?"

She was silent for a while thinking her answer out, "That time with you was the best time of my life. I have never been close to anyone especially a boy who is like me. I see so much of me in you. How I was in the beginning. The hope in your eyes, even though you won't admit it, that was me in the beginning. My first time in this place. They give you the meds and release you and you think it could get better. They don't tell you that you're still going to struggle and that those people out there fix nothing. Before you know it you're here over and over and over. It becomes a revolving door. Sometimes you want to die, and sometimes you just want the pain to end."

Absentmindedly, Angel rubbed where she had been cutting on her arm. The visible scars were the shallow ones and he knew the deep ones, the ones that made her leave on a stretcher were deeper under the bandages. James had never actually self-harmed before, but he understood how it was done and why. Emotional pain is impossible to deal with, what is physical pain to emotional turmoil?

She continued, "I was so happy James. Your hand in mine. For a moment everything else disappeared. The pain was bearable, and for a moment that hole in my soul began to fill, and then the night ended. I realized that you have people in your life. A girlfriend. That hole in my soul opened once again bigger than before. I let myself be vulnerable when I told myself never again."

"Angel—" James stopped for a moment. What could he say? He loved his girlfriend but there was a part of him that had feelings for this girl that was so new and exciting. It would only be widening the gap in her soul if he continued to press his life into her own. Then he did something he would regret for the rest of his miserable existence—he kissed Angel with a passion that could rival any kiss he ever gave Victoria. Angel returned the kiss and for a while they became one.

When the moment of passion passed Angel put her hand on James' face. "I was hoping you felt the same way. There is something I need to ask you. I have to know that what you feel for me is real."

"I think what I just did was enough was it not? What more can I do that will make me miserable that I have a girlfriend, but I'm falling in love with someone else?"

Angel looked at the door for the moment and when she believed the coast was clear, she got up to the cabinet adjacent to her bed. James could see that she was peeling back part of one of the shelves looking for something. When she returned, she sat on the bed revealing a razor blade.

"Is that," he stopped to point at the razor blade, "what you used to cut on yourself?"

"Not this one exactly, but one like it. I know you understand the emotional pain. The need to want to die. You know it all too well. It's not gone is it?"

"I have changed Angel, what happened to you—"

"You can tell yourself that you want to change but search your soul right now. If you truly believe that you're over that feeling of wanting to die, you get up right now and tell the nurses that I have another razor blade," she said.

James could feel it creeping back in. The monster. The darkness that was there the since he got to the ward. He had pushed it away by saying *"things can get better, and they will get better."* The darkness new the truth and so did Angel. You can't change. Not in this life because once the darkness gets ahold of you it never let's go. Angel was proof that the darkness always wins.

"You feel it don't you. The dark companion, that's what I call it. It demands payment. Blood its best medicine. You don't need to cut deep, all you need is to bleed."

Angel handed the razor blade to James who took it starting at the crossroads that he now found himself. On the one road was Victoria and his family, the people that loved him more than anything in this world. The other road was darker and at the end of it was the emotional pain of his depression. James had a choice. He could leave this room, Angel, and the darkness behind forever. But the feeling. The need. The dark companion. Angel was right, it demanded payment, it demanded to be felt before it could leave.

With the razor blade in hand he slashed a deep incision on his right forearm. The rush of blood became euphoric, and he could feel the darkness fading, but it was not completely gone. Blood ran down his arm and it took some clean bandage the nurses had given Angel for her own wounds and cleaned up James arm by applying pressure. Before long the cut was not bleeding. The pain was so real that the emotional pain began to fade, a serene level of peace overcame James.

"That was an amazing experience. I have never felt the darkness leave me so quickly. The pain was nothing I couldn't handle. I could do that a hundred more times and not feel it," James said looking up at Angel. He kissed her again passionately. She was the first person to ever take away the pain. James' life would never be the same, but he had no idea what he had begun with Angel. The darkness always wins.

"This is only the beginning, James. We will embrace the darkness together."

Part Eight

JAMES WAS A DIFFERENT person when he opened his eyes the next morning. Over the course of twenty-four hours he had gone from being open to having a mental illness and wanting to be better for Victoria and the ones that loved him, to letting go of the darkness, possibly for good. James could not explain the rush of adrenaline that came from self-harming. For the first time he had embraced the darkness as a friend instead of an enemy. He had found his religion and the woman who understood the dark side that James hid from the world.

Overnight everything had changed. He had promised Angel that he would cut off his family from visiting. They would only make things difficult, she told him that they wanted to change what was unchangeable. They would never understand what they both would have to go through to stay alive. At the time, his promises to Angel were very real, but that was the adrenaline of cutting on his skin had given him. Now his resolve was not good.

There was an overwhelming feeling that he was falling for Angel, or at least the part of himself that Angel helped come alive. Victoria was the opposite of Angel; she was the life and the light. This made him laugh because before last night he had thought Angel was the light. That is exactly what it was like now for James. Angel pulling him to the darkness and Victoria pulling to the light. James had no idea which side was going to win.

As James began his morning routine, for the first time he really noticed his roommate. He was a large man, there was no other way to describe it. Since coming into the ward, he had made no effort to change, and now in the light of the morning James could see the man's ass crack peaking from his hospital gown. It was not the best sight to wake to but pushing this out of his mind he thought about the day ahead. For now, he would call his mother and Victoria and let them know that he was not feeling up to visitors. He had come up with the excuse that they had visited him every day since coming, and they needed some time away from a place such as the ward.

James wanted to be next to Angel all day, as she made him feel alive and the darkness she brought to his life. He loved Victoria, he decided, but he needed Angel right now. He got dressed in his normal clothes but made sure to wear his favorite hoodie jacket, he would all day, so that it would hide the cut that was now just a scar. The cut had not been deep, and there was no blood coming from the wound. Now it was just starting to show tissue but hiding it was the best thing in place like the ward.

It was still early when James made his way out into the ward's common room. He waved at the nurses at the station and made his way to the phone. The first call was to his mother, he had forgotten the time of day and it was his father not his mother that answered.

He told his father all that he had rehearsed, and his father agreed that giving his mother the day off would be good for her. James could tell in his father's voice that the less his mother visited was good in his eyes. His next phone call was to Victoria, who was up and heading to church when she answered her cell phone. Victoria was less agreeable about the free time.

"You can spend the day with your mom. You and I both know that you need time with your mother before you go back to school. I will still be here for a few more days. Please, I feel bad," James said.

He knew Victoria better than anyone and what he said hit home, "You'll be okay?"

"I promise I will."

"Okay, I love you James."

"I love you too," he returned. A pain of guilt hit his stomach. What he said was true, he loved Victoria but the other part of his life, the part on the ward was changing him and he had to know her more than seeing Victoria.

With the calls done he had time before breakfast to wait for Angel. There was no doubt in his mind that they would be spending the day together—they had made those plans before James left the room. An excitement came over James. He wanted to know more about embracing the darkness because overnight since he left Angel's room it had crept back into his soul. It was worse than ever, the darkness mixed with emotional pain. He wanted it gone again.

Relief washed over him when Angel took her place on the opposite side of the dining table, he was sitting at thinking of her. James could see a strange difference in the woman that almost a week earlier when they had met, she seemed weak and fragile. A new sense of self and self-confidence had taken over her. As if the events of the night before had awakened something. James could not place it, but breakfast with all the patients and nurses was not the place to ask questions.

In their usual manner they ate in silence, but the pair exchanged looks that made James feel at ease, he even saw her smile for once. They finished breakfast and Angel made her way out to the atrium where they could be alone and in silence. After a spell, James followed her.

Angel was the first to talk, "How do you feel this morning?"

"Better, and at the same time worse. I felt so amazing last night, but since returning to my room I could feel the darkness slowly creeping back inside me," he said pointing to his heart.

"That tends to happen. What you had was a small taste of what can make the darkness go away. The bad part? It always comes back stronger. Sometimes you have to cut deeper to make it go away longer," she responded.

"I wanted to ask you something," James said reluctantly, "What are you in this place for?"

"The doctors call it schizoaffective disorder. It's a combination of schizophrenia and bipolar disorder. I have had it since the doctors first gave me a diagnosis in the beginning. The doctors say it's incurable."

Angel paused for a moment taking a razor blade from a hiding place just behind the trees. The girl had blades hidden everywhere.

"Here give me your right hand."

James gave his hand to her, but she was interested in his forearm. Angel pushed the sleeve of his hoodie up to his elbow. With a look of devotion, she brushed her fingers over the forming scar, and her touch ignited a fire inside.

"You heal quickly, that's good. This next cut will have to be deeper," she said.

James stopped to look around, "How are you going to keep the nurses from seeing the blood. If it bleeds through my jacket—"

She reaches into the pocket of her own jacket and pulled out a wad to toilet paper.

"It will be deep but not so deep that it will need medical attention. It will be just deep enough for the pain to go away for a while. You want to do this, right?" she looked at him almost possessing him to answer.

"Yes, I do."

Angel took her left-hand caressing James' cheek soothing him before kissing him. With her right hand she made an expert slice just under the scar from the night before, she was so much better at this than James. It was an invigorating sensation. Like the night before the darkness faded but faster. Then Angel did something unexpected, with her finger she gathered up some blood using her tongue to clean her finger. James was clearly freaked, and it showed. Angel said nothing at first cleaning up the remainder of the blood and making the wound stop.

"What the hell was that?" he asked her.

"Sorry. That was weird I know. I just wondered what your blood would taste like and it was like most blood, metallic tasting. I tried my own once and it had this same metallic taste. Yours was not that different. You feel better, though right?"

"Loads better actually. You're very good with a razor."

"It's sort of a specialty of mine," she showed James her wrists. "I have learned how to draw just enough blood to make the emotional pain go away for a long period of time."

"Can I ask you something without you getting mad at me?"

"Depends. Go ahead," she said.

"I get the appeal of small cuts on your arm. It takes away the pain for a while and it feels good. But why did you slit your wrists?"

For a moment James could see something in Angel's eyes, but it was only for a moment like it was anger but it was gone as quickly, "the pain that you feel, the smaller the cut the less emotional pain. Eventually you have to cut deeper. Your veins are the best place to feel good."

Angel traced with her fingers on James' right wrist and he could tell that she was imagining not James' wrists but her own. There was a darkness in her as she looked at his wrists. When their eyes locked again it was like their dark passengers were saying hello to one another. It was both scary and energizing.

The pair spent their morning in the atrium lost in their own little heaven on the ward. Only once were they interrupted by the nurses and it was only to administer medication to the both of them. It was not hard to notice that Angel was on more medication than James, but he already knew she had spent years in this life.

Was this my future? Pill after pill and still no way to end this darkness.

Angel broke into his thoughts. They were both sitting on the cold cement benches with their heads next to one another their cheeks touching, and here and there they would ask one another questions, and then the two would two would go silent. It was always how they communicated with one another.

"When did you start to feel the darkness for the first time?" she asked James.

"I was maybe fourteen. I had no idea what it was at the time. I always thought that my behavior was a result of teenage angst. I started to ditch school with my cousin on a weekly basis to smoke weed and play video games. It was the only thing that got me out in the world. If I wasn't ditching, I would spend days at a time in bed staring at the ceiling lost in my thoughts. I could never get ahold of it for a long time. It was a part of me, but eventually I found my way out of the fog. My junior year was better, and I was more active in social things. It never fit me though and I always felt like an outsider. I would spend a lot of my time with my music in my ear, even among my friends or I spent time in the computer lab playing video games."

Pausing for a moment he looked at Angel for the first time since he started to answer her questions. Angel was hanging on is every word and her smile gave him the courage to continue to talk.

"My senior year was the worse. I was working a janitor's job three days a week, but the pay was practically nothing. I spent the money on useless things like DVD's. Things someone doesn't actually need. I always had trouble with money. I graduated high school, but it was barely. I went straight into the work force, but I could never really hold down a job. Eventually the darkness came back into my life, and it always took over. I spend just as much time not working as I did working even for only being twenty-two."

He had been talking with taking little breath and for a moment he stopped letting his breathing catch up.

"About a year and a half ago I walked into my last job and quit. No rhyme or reason. I just didn't want to be. At some level is it was the darkness. I could not function with my darkness and being myself outside in the world. The darkness has won ever since. I have been depressed. Suicidal. On the edge for so long. About six months ago my father made me work for my uncle at his business. He is a computer engineer, but I was mostly working grunt office work when I could work. Most days I would call in and he would get mad. He wanted me to find direction."

For the third time he had to pause to catch his breath.

"The one positive thing for me since I quit that job was Victoria. I was sitting at a coffee shop playing a video game on my laptop when she came up to me and started to talk to me. She was so bold, and she always knew what she wanted. She actually asked me out on our first date. Vic became my beacon of light, and for a while the darkness was gone, but she had school down south. It worked okay for the first year but since summer ended it has been different."

"Then on this last Halloween the darkness took me over again, stronger than ever before. It told me that I had to kill myself. That this was not the life that I was to lead. My family found me in time, and I was in the hospital, but they released me after signing a paper that I wouldn't harm myself. I saw a psychiatrist but that was useless as all he did was give me antidepressants and told me to see him in three months. A few weeks later, here I am."

Angel had been resting her head on his lap listening quietly to James' story. She seemed to be lost in her own thoughts, or maybe she was connecting her own story to the one James just told. It was a while before she spoke again.

"You still love her, don't you?"

James knew who she was referring too, and it was hard to speak the truth. Victoria was the light in his life, and he needed her. Angel was the understanding of a different kind, and maybe the closest thing to understanding his darkness. "She is a major part of my life Angel," he said quickly, "But you're becoming a big part as well. Victoria would never understand the dark parts of the life we live. Do you hate me for wanting her and you?"

"I get. Anyway, we are stuck in here and she is out there. There is nothing she can do to help you at all. Not in here."

James pondered that for a long moment. Angel had, for a fleeting moment, took away the pain. The last cut had been a bit deeper and Angel warned him that it was a temporary thing. The darkness would come back. She was not wrong. Thinking about his life from age fourteen to twenty-two was allowing the darkness to make its way back. There was something wrong with Angel's logic.

Yes, the darkness always came back, but he had never used self-harm to push the darkness away in the past, it went away on its own. In fact, it was always something changing in his life that pushed the darkness away. The last time it was Victoria, and though he wanted to die just days ago he could feel the nagging feeling that he never really wanted to die, it was just something to do to end the darkness.

There was the other side of this logic. Even with Victoria in his life he had succumbed to the darkness. So, what was right and what was wrong? Cutting on his arm had been exhilarating, at least for a while. Even now as the physical pain subsided, he could feel the slow creeping of the darkness, but it was so much stronger. If James really thought about it, when he woke up this morning he felt like crap. It was the events still fresh in his mind that was making him feel good right now, but he wondered how long it would last.

Absentmindedly James began to rub his fingers over his scars as Angel was lost staring at the sky above. How had he gotten here? What was it about this girl that changed something in him? Why was he mesmerized by her every action and words? The night before he had cut on his skin without much thoughts of the consequences. What if the doctors found out and he would be here for a longer than he wanted? Was this what Angel had wanted? He looked down at Angel and for the first time he was seeing her in a different light.

Part Nine

IT WAS THE LATE morning time and Angel was put in the afternoon group therapy. James was offered a spot in the current session. Apparently, the nurses took notice in how close the two were getting and were taking opportunities to separate them. James minded little, some time away from Angel would help him clear his head.

Group was interesting for the first time. James never understood how people could sit in a circle and share their thoughts on their illness. James was more attentive this time and he did love to hear the stories of how his fellow mental illness sufferers were feeling. James had always fashioned himself as someone different, a complete outsider in any world, but he was feeling a kindred spirit with these people.

He was only a few days into believing that something was terribly wrong inside him and now he was using self-harm as a coping mechanism. Even without James feeling up to sharing, he had spent so much time that morning sharing his life story with Angel, but as people shared, he felt more connected to these people. The only downside of his time at group was that Ryan was a part of this session. It made him smile how similar the two were after hearing him talk about his own experiences, after the meeting he would learn just how much.

When then the group therapy session came to its merciful end, the mixed members of the group therapy session all began their ritual of leaving or getting ready to leave. James lingered for a moment because he knew the next thing would be seeing Angel. It was worrying James that he was weary to see her. Rubbing the place over his hoodie where he had cut on skin earlier made the darkness that was creeping into his life seem real. It was amazing that the night before the darkness was just something that was there, sure it felt like it was controlling James at times, but this was different. Every time he pushed the darkness away with cutting on his skin, the darkness took more hold on him and it was controlling every thought.

James noticed that he was not the only one that had decided to linger. Ryan was sitting just across from him and most of the room was empty. James' first thought that this was going to end the way that all their interactions had up to this point—in some sort of pissing contest. It was far from what he wanted and so he got up, but Ryan mirrored the movement.

"I wanted to talk you," he said to James' who began retreating back.

He turned around to face Ryan, "Not today my friend. Not in the mood."

"I'm not in the mood to get into anything other than talking to you, we need to talk about Angel."

This made James stop in his tracks, he didn't know what to say. He had no idea Ryan even knew Angel. If he thought about it, and he decided he would, it made sense. Since the beginning he could tell that Ryan was a regular. The way he pranced around like he ran the place was the attitude of someone who knew this place often. It made sense then that the two would have crossed paths at least once. James turned around finding the closest chair and motioned Ryan to sit.

"How do you know Angel?"

"Come on James, you're a smart man. Look, I will always be a regular here and so is she, let's leave it at that," he said. "There is something about Angel that you don't know. You're not the first person that has been enamored by her charms. She is an amazing woman and there is something about her that draws people her. She has this magnetism that is irresistible."

He paused shifting in his seat so that he could look James in the eyes before continuing.

"I met her about a two years ago. We were both young. I was in here because, well you know my anger. When you mix that with borderline personality disorder you get the chaotic life that I live. You're lucky, you know, you have it easier than most," he said. For a moment he looked sheepish as if he was trying to make a point not rehash old things. "Angel had already been a regular a few times when I met her. She was so quiet, but she had this thing about her that made me want to know her."

Ryan was lost for a moment no doubt trying to work out his memories of Angel, "We just started clicking on day one. We talked and I had never connected to someone exactly like me in every way. She said that her diagnosis was borderline personality disorder, and it was amazing to find someone with the same diagnosis. I was very new to life with a diagnosis, but Angel seemed to know everything."

James got up not wanting to hear more. The story Ryan was telling. It was James' story with Angel but with slight differences. This hurt his mind, but he sat down next to Ryan again. He did not want to not know this story, but there was no walking away.

Ryan continued, "It all sound familiar doesn't it?" James stayed silent. "It was slow at first, she began telling me about the darkness. This thing inside people like us that takes over completely. I had felt it so many times in my life, but I could never quite understand what it was until Angel described it to me. It was turning on a light type of feeling. The darkness was truly real, and she knew how to take the emotional pain away."

Ryan turn over both his arms so that his forearm was showing. He could see plenty of cuts, some deeper than others. But it was the ones on his wrist that got James attention. These were deep and James was surprised that Ryan was still alive.

"She asked me one night what I was willing to do. I told her anything and I meant it. I don't blame her for what happened, I knew what it meant, but she was invigorating to me. I did what she asked, and she left me there laying on the floor as if I didn't matter anymore. I made it to the nurses in time. And after? She acted as if nothing had happened. We have not said two words to one another since that day."

He got up and began to walk away before turning. "I'm not saying that she is still that same vindictive person that I knew then, but we are not so different you and I. Angel can be the most amazing person in this world, but that darkness you feel, that she says you feel, did you ever think that it was something she made up?"

With that Ryan left leaving James to ponder. At some level he wished that Ryan was lying but there were parts of his story that matched his own. The first thing to unpack was the strangest part of Ryan's story. Angel had said that she had borderline personality disorder to Ryan. James was no expert, but did people tend to change a diagnosis? It was possible he thought, but the truth was glaring. Angel had told Ryan that they were the same, just like Angel had done with James.

The hardest thing was what Ryan had said to him about the darkness. It was true, the darkness at this moment seemed real. Just like before Angel. But, as he had already figured that out, it was never overwhelming like it was now. In the less than twenty-four hours he had changed. He had let Angel help him control the darkness, but was he really controlling it or just pushing it away to deal with another day?

The only other explanation was that Ryan was jealous of the time he had been spending with Angel. The mea culpa that Ryan spewed was just him trying to confuse what was happening with Angel. *No, Angel is trying to save me.* It was clear that Ryan was the enemy, not Angel. There was no way everything that happened with Ryan and James that all of a sudden, he wanted to help James. By the time he left the group therapy room, he was convinced that Angel was there for him—and no one else.

It was late afternoon into early evening on the ward and James was quietly reading a book laying on the sofa. Angel had to meet with the psychiatrist about her incident from the day before leaving James with a lot of time to think. He had wanted to do nothing but read, because reading was a great distraction from his own thoughts.

When his mind slipped into thought rather than the book that was in front of him, he continued the inner monologue about what he was going to do. He was just two full days on the ward from having a chance to leave this place for good. James thought about Victoria and moving down to Los Angeles with her for good. But the darkness wanted something different—Angel and her self-harming way. She was a drug and he could feel that the darkness was back, feeding him thoughts wanting to be pushed away again. It was a craving, and he knew now where Angel kept her razors. At least one. He could do it without her, but there was a side, the darkness, that needed her there next to him.

With his right hand on his heart he could feel the increase in his heartbeat as he waited for Angel to return to him. It was so fast at times he wondered to himself if it was a good thing to have his heart racing. When Angel returned, she found James right away and sat next to him on the couch.

James got up closing the book he was reading. He noticed right away that Angel's mood from this morning, once of positivity, had been replaced by something darker. Her meeting did not go well.

"Things didn't go well?"

She shot him a look, "What do you think?" she stopped, giving him an apologetic look. "Sorry. It's just the doctors want to keep me here for the long-term and move me to a state facility in the future. They won't tell me when I can leave. I guess trying to cut on myself again was wrong. It's not like it was deep enough to kill me. It never is, you get it right?"

"I do," he said back.

"I don't know. It pisses me off, but this is my life. I'm tired of this shit," she said. Without a word she walked off to her room leaving James with only the darkness as his companion.

Dinner that night was a solo affair as he did not see Angel again that night. James was relieved in a way, but he hated the fact that Angel had asked him to skip his visits and then shut herself in her room. He thought about visiting her like he did once before, but that was hard to do. His roommate was more active than the night before and it would be impossible to sneak out without him knowing.

After dinner he joined the group of patients for another movie night and before long, he was lying in bed letting sleep overcome him. He could feel he darkness at his fingertips.

Part Ten

THE NIGHTMARE HAD BEEN bad, one of the worst James had ever experienced. James was walking but he knew not where. There were no walls, no floors, and no people—just darkness and nothing more. His hands tried to reach out and grasp something, but it grabbed nothing. In the distance he could see something, no he could feel someone. James was too far away to see, but as he moved closer the world became clearer.

As if by magic, the ward appeared out of the darkness, and he could see the familiar corridor leading to the common room. He was walking from his own room. When he arrived at the nurse's station it was empty. No people, computers, or anything—nothing but emptiness. Then the darkness came behind from far into the distance of the nurse's station pushing him forward.

For a moment he began to slip but caught himself in time. He bent down to feel for what he was slipping on. When he brought his hand back to his face, he could smell exactly what the substance was—the metallic smell of blood and it was still warm. But who's? The common room was much like it always was, very pink and couches everywhere. Now they were newly bought furniture. When he would stop, he could feel these things disappearing as the darkness began pushing him towards whatever was in in front of him. As he started down the corridor a smell reached his nose and it was like wet metal. He had smelt it once before, it was the blood, and it was getting stronger with every step.

He knew the only way to get away from the smell was to continue on and the darkness continued to push him every time that he made the decision to stop. It was a pushy darkness, but he did not want it to overtake him. He knew that allowing the darkness to overcome him was a bad idea and so he continued down the path walking a different faster pace. It was taking an eternity to walk down the corridor, and it worried him that the opened doors he passed, places where patients should have been, were empty. He was alone in this strange place.

He thought about what was ahead and with that thought he heard something for the first time, his name—*James*. The voice was familiar, but it was also unknown to him. It was beckoning to him. No, it was pleading with him—*James, please.* Quickening his pace, he tried to reach the voice, but as he did this the darkness took ahold of his arms and held him in place. The more he fought the more the darkness consumed him. When he relaxed the darkness did the same and when James became completely motionless it let go. The darkness was in control here and it was not ready for James to see what was calling him forward.

At a slower place he continued down the path, but this time there was a door open in front of him was illuminating and inviting. He stopped at the door and he let out a gasp. It was him lying in a bed, not unlike the one that you find in a hospital. He recognized the people around him. Victoria holding his hand and crying. His mother holding his other hand crying her eyes out as well. His family was all around him and a doctor, one he had never met and had no face was talking to his father. At first, he could not here the words, but as he moved closer, he heard a single sentence.

"There is nothing we can do at this point. James won't be a part of this world for much longer."

He looked at himself. This version of himself was different. Skinnier and clearly older. He looked at Victoria and with a surprise she was pregnant and had a ring on her finger. James had obviously tried to fix his life but failed.

This version of himself was something different and with a closer examination he could see the many scars on his arms. As he reached out, and the darkness overcame the scene. With a push from his tormentor, he was back in the corridor.

James tried to shake his head in hopes to wake himself up, but it was no use. He knew he had no choice but to continue. *James, please help me.* The voice was getting stronger and so he did what the darkness bade him and moved forward. The next door the he happened upon was open and illuminated like the last. He stopped in front of this door and it was another version of himself.

James was alone, and everything was dark around him. A small light was an illumination of a television screen and he was playing a video game. He didn't look unhappy, but he was not happy. He was older like before. His hair was longer, and he was sporting a very unity beard. As James came closer to this version of himself, he could see pill bottles all around, but they had all their contents. He could smell metal mixed with someone who had not bathed in a few days. This was a sad version of himself but one that he could see happening. It was clear that Victoria was no longer in his life, and it felt like it was most likely for the best. He could see that while he was playing a video game there was blood dripping from a fresh cut on his arm. This was a version of what life could be. Video games and trying to take the pain away and not much else to note.

The darkness wanted him to keep moving, and so it pushed him from the scene in this room and back into the hallway.

He could not help but yell out, "Why are you doing this to me?"

The darkness was quiet but at that moment he heard it clearer than ever. *James.* It was a voice he knew all too well.

It was eerie, and he knew not how to respond. His only action was moving forward, he would learn soon about the voice. When James came to the next open door, he was weary about what he would see. It was a surprise.

It was James and Victoria. They were living in a city from what it looked like outside the window of the room. They were dancing and as he entered the room, he could see they were in a small kitchen. James had his arms around Victoria and on the counter were vegetables on a cutting board, some cut and some waiting. James had clearly interrupted what Victoria was doing and the look on James' face was something that he had never seen — true happiness. Victoria was his light and his center. Unlike the James' in the other rooms this one had only two visible scars on his arms, and he only noticed because his eyes were drawn to there by the darkness. He only knew them because both had them in the same place. He looked down at his own arm where those two scars were trying to heal themselves.

He was getting angry now, "Why are you showing me this!"

The darkness was silent, and he could see out the window the skyline of New York City. His dream place to move. James dropped to his knees letting his arms hit the floor. Tears began to fall down his face creating small droplets on the tile floor. This was a fake reality. One that he would or never could see in the real world. Without the help of the darkness he left this room. Not before taking one last look at the happiness in the eyes of this version of himself.

He was back in the corridor and this time he was closer to what was waiting for him since the beginning. He knew, or maybe it was the darkness telling him so, that there was only one stop left and it would not be a pretty sight.

Walking down the corridor he could finally see the door and as he approached, and he heard the worst blood curling scream he had ever heard. He ran into the room in time to see himself laying on the floor. This version of James lay in a puddle of his own blood as it came gushing out of his wrists. His eyes had rolled over and all he could see was the whites of his eyes. The James before him was not older, and this was not in some distant future. This was the James of now.

He looked down with horror as blood continued to run from his wrists. He looked behind him and the trail that he was following was not of this James before him, but the one who had been walking all this time toward his future. His own wrists were cut and bleeding profusely. He heard a blood curling scream escape again this time from his own lips as the James on floor sat up.

"Help me, James."

Part Eleven

JAMES WOKE SCREAMING, though unintentionally. It was a long time before he came to his senses about where he was and that it was all a dream. He looked around but the world through his eyes was unfocused. His overly large roommate was staring at him when the world came back into focus and the look on his face was as if he had seen a ghost.

"Sorry, I was having a bad dream," James said quickly.

His roommate looked unconvinced and was looking toward the door to the outside before he spoke.

"You were doing more than having a bad dream," he said in a shaky voice, "you were talking and screaming for a while. I didn't know if I should wake you or what was wrong with you."

James shook his head trying to refocus. He had never been one to remember his dreams, and even the ones that he did remember were never so vivid. For some reason he was remembering everything from the dream. The blood. The rooms. The futures and more than anything himself telling, well, himself, to help himself. What had any of it meant? It was a mystery and it was bothering James. It was making his roommate more nervous by the second the more that he sat there not saying anything.

"I'm all right. It was just a dream. Dreams can't hurt you," he said to his roommate.

Reluctantly his roommate turned his back on James and laid back down, but he was sure he was far from falling asleep. He had a feeling that his roommate was now scared of him. James got up and made his way to their small shared bathroom, splashing some cold water on his face. What he told his roommate was far from what he believed. When his eyes had opened it had all felt real and his scream had been because he thought his own wrists really were bleeding. He looked down to the cut-less and non-bleeding wrists that were his own.

He was looking at his reflection in the mirror. The dark circles that always engulfed his eyes were the worst he had ever seen. He looked as if he had not slept for weeks, and he felt the darkness even stronger now that he was staring at himself. He racked his brain, trying to figure out what day it was, because his life on the ward was starting to feel like a life sentence.

He knew he came to the hospital on a Tuesday night, two days before Thanksgiving because he had attempted to take his life with sleeping pills. Wednesday was the first full day on the ward. Thursday, Friday, and Saturday had all passed meaning that yesterday was Sunday. He had been on the ward for five days. He was about to start the sixth day — Monday. So much had happened since then and he was weary about the dream. It came flooding back.

Could it have just been a dream? Something that his mind created to show that from here he could go down many dark paths or he could change for the better? Remembering how happy he looked in an apartment in New York City quickly became the center of his thoughts. That James was so much different than the one staring back at him now. James could not remember a time in his life where he had ever been that happy, at least not at first. Then he remembered he happiest day in his life.

James had been sitting much like he did every day for the last few months in the later afternoons, on his computer playing his favorite massive multiplayer online role-playing game at his local Starbucks. He had been nursing for over an hour an iced passion tea, his favorite and frequent drink. The barista that worked the afternoon shift was a friend and manager, so he often got free drinks. He usually avoided people retreating to the cornet table far from anyone, but the coffee shop had been unusually busy even for the afternoon on a Wednesday. It was an unusually hot day outside and so people ran to shelter inside the coffee shop.

James was happy, which was a rare thing for him. Life had been getting some normalcy. He was working a few hours at his uncle's office and then he would spend the afternoons and evenings here, using the free internet to play his games. He was not content with his life, and things had been going horribly wrong for a while, but it was a nice summer day and he was not laying in the darkness of his room consumed by his thoughts.

He noticed Victoria when she came into the coffee shop, how could he not. Victoria's long hair was straight and went down to her lower back. She was tall, a bit shorter than James and had the most incredible legs he had ever seen. It was a hot day and so she was wearing short shorts. Her eyes were hazel, and she had the most perfect shaped face—a little round but perfection. None of that mattered because it was her smile that caught James' attention. It was the most beautiful smile he had ever seen.

Victoria was with someone, her sister by the looks and they were deep in conversation, so James went back to ignoring the world. *Girls like that don't go out with geeky guys like me.*

James was deep in concentration of his game before he realized the girl that he was checking out was now sitting across from him. James had been sitting at a small table with his gaming headphones on, and the table was fit for maybe two people. She was staring at him and smiling that breathtaking smile. She seemed to be patiently waiting. He looked around the coffee shop. Her sister was sitting on a couch on her phone across the coffee shop, but this girl was just sitting across from him gazing with those beautiful eyes at James. He realized at once that she was sipping on his favorite drink—a passion sweet tea.

He took his gaming headphones off his ears.

"I was wondering how long it was going to take you to look up, some game I take it," she said with a smile.

"Coffee shop is kind of crowded today isn't it?" he answered back.

"True," she said looking around, "there aren't many empty seats and you looked so lonely here and I thought, if there is a place to sit so why not here." She smiled again at James and it was intoxicating.

"I feel like the luckiest guy in the world."

"You are the luckiest guy, you just don't know it yet," she said back.

It was the best afternoon James had ever spent in his life. It was not long before he forgot about the game he was playing. He was enamored by how this young woman talked and how she commanded the attention of anyone that was she was talking to, and there was not a man in that coffee shop that day that wanted to be where James now found himself.

"The girl with you," he motioned to the girl on the couch. "She looks familiar."

"My sister? You know her from somewhere?"

"I didn't know it was your sister," he said. He thought for a moment. "Yeah, she went out with a friend of mine, she went to the rival school. I take it you went there as well."

"So, you know Seth. That's the guy she dated for three years of high school. Dude was kind of a dick."

James had to laugh at this because he knew it well, "Yeah well most high school jocks are like that for the most part. He's an okay guy. I've known his since we were kids.

He lived not far from me. Too bad you didn't go to my high school."

"You never know. Spencer and I could have gone to different schools. How do you know I'm not still in high school?"

"You're roughly the same age as me maybe younger but out of high school, and someone like you I would have remembered," he said back.

She smiled that smile that made his heart beat just a little more than before. "Well, you're right. Not that we are the same age and I did go to a different high school. Spencer recognized you," she said looking back at sister. "She said that while you were not a jock you were popular with kids."

"Really? She said that?" he said.

It was a funny thing but one that he had heard before. But it was far from the truth. Sure, he was well known. He was smart. Relatively good looking. Well he was highly intelligent. He was well on his way his freshman year to being top of his class and valedictorian, before the depression took over. James decided that he wanted to work instead of going to college after high school.

In school James was popular because he was smart, but he never felt a part of anything when it came to school. He preferred to be alone and playing video games to actual human conversation. Still, when he felt like it, he could be the most social person on the planet. Apparently, that gave him a reputation.

"I guess she was right. If it makes her feel any better, I think Seth is a dick as well."

The afternoon passed rather quickly. Too quickly for James' liking and if her sister had not been there, they might have more time together. He was trying to find an opening to ask her out. Victoria had taken James by surprise. He had never been around someone so forward and it was intimidating to a point that that he was willing to let this girl get away — *she would be one hell of girl to say this is the one that got away.*

"Well, I guess this is goodbye. You're the most forward woman I have ever met."

"I guess this is goodbye James," she got up from her chair. She paused for a moment staring into James' eyes almost daring him to ask her out, but in the same moment she decided. "Give me your phone," he handed it to her. "Here is my number. I expect to get a call from you soon, don't wait too long something this good doesn't last forever."

Setting his phone down, she walked away. James called her that night and she asked him out for a date. They were together ever since.

James came back to reality as he could hear his roommate hastily getting ready for his day. James wanted to go back to bed and stay there for the remainder of his time in this place. His life was so messy at the moment. It was worse than when he had entered the ward. How had things gotten so messy that he was now making everyone he loved unhappy? His mother had to live with the fact that her son wanted nothing more than to be out of this world. His family now lived with the reality that this might not be a one-time thing for James — that someday he might succeed in taking his life for good.

Then there was Victoria. All his thoughts after last night went back to him. Even when James was depressed, and he had been depressed for several months, his girlfriend had been his rock. The reason to live, but he had tried to take his life regardless of the positive influence of Victoria. He didn't deserve Victoria and he wanted nothing more than to end things. *She deserves better.*

The last few days he had let the darkness take control of his life, and while he had also seen some of the darkness go away with the self-harming sessions with Angel, it was clear he was not getting better, only worse. What was keeping his so attached to Angel was the self-harm and taking away the darkness for a fleeting moment. It felt so good in the moment, but at this moment the darkness was more in his life than ever before.

He could feel it from the tips of his fingers to his toes. It was a part of who he was, and who he would always be. This darkness would always be a part of his life and he was allowed to be happy for moments but that was it. It felt so much to James like a parasite. How could he keep going at this pace? Maybe that was what he dreams were telling him. That in this life there is no future, and when he saw happiness with Victoria it was all a lie.

Part Twelve

JAMES WAS PURPOSELY LATE for breakfast, much to the chagrins of the nurses who were ready to be done with the morning rush to feed the masses. With a little sass, the morning nurse put a tray in front of him. The dining area and the common room were completely empty, exactly as he had hoped it would be. Most of the patients were most likely going about their day.

James was not a religious man. He believed that there was something out there in the world to believe in for most people, but people like him, who always struggled with darkness, it was hopeless. Broken people couldn't be saved. He remembered that he read in some religions, that James trying to take his life was a sin, and unforgivable. This was the one area he had always argued with Victoria who was deeply religious and so was her family. When they talked about the future it would always end with James saying that if they had kids, he would let her decide their religious beliefs, but he would also give them a choice when they were older. Now, James was not sure that he would have a relationship with Victoria.

The real reason James has chosen to be late for breakfast was to avoid Angel. It was all too much with the dream playing in a constant loop in his mind. By now he hoped to shake the dream, but it only gotten worse and it was burning itself into his memory. This dream had significance, James knew this, but what did it truly mean? He had no idea.

It was lucky then that after breakfast it was time for James to see the psychiatric doctor. He figured at the very least he could ask questions about the significant of dreams without actually telling the doctor about the dream. No one needed to know about the darkness, and he knew it would only work against his plans of being out of the psych ward.

So, with a plan in mind he knocked on the door of the psych doctor's office, and with permission entered siting opposite of the doctor, it was scary to James how much he had the routine of the ward down.

"James, it's good to see you again. I know we talked a lot about your acceptance of your medications and more importantly your diagnosis last time. How's that coming along?" he asked.

"It's going as well as it could. I told my girlfriend and my family my plans and that I want to work towards the future. Not sure what they believe but it's a step in a direction."

"That's good. You're right about it being a step in a direction, hopefully the right one," he responded.

"I think it is," he said to the doctor. James hated lying to anyone. It was not how he was raised, but this was about his long-term stay in this place. "I did have a question."

"About?"

"Dreams. I have been having, well let's just say nightmares about things that I feel I have no control over," he said. James was surprised that he was able to articulate even this, the dream was so much more. Control seemed like the right phrase.

"They're more like are very vivid nightmares, almost real," he continued.

"Well, not being a sleep doctor that specializes in dreams, I want you to know that before I respond," he said. Then he continued, "From what I know about nightmares is that they usually manifest when someone is feeling fear, anxiety or even terror in their life. Given the events of the past week, it would not be uncommon to have a nightmare. There is a curiosity that I have about the distinction you made. You said the nightmare was vivid almost real. What was it about?"

This is where James knew it would get tricky. If he told him that he woke up screaming in terror because he thought that his wrists, like in the dream, were bleeding, he might be in here longer. James thought about what to tell and what not to tell, and this is what he came up with.

"I was dreaming that I was walking down this corridor, it looked a lot like the ward. I could hear screaming and I tried to reach that place, but I was unable for a time. When I did, I woke up. That's all I could remember. It did seem real though,' he said.

The doctor began to examine James, and how he was acting quite anxious with his hands which had not stopped moving since he began talking about the nightmares. The doctor saw how nervous and sweaty James was and how at time he could not meet his eye. It worried the doctor, but he could tell that if there was more, he was not going to get anything else out of him.

"Freud believed that nightmares and dreams come from your unconscious mind and that they manifest in what the dreamer's secret fears or even your desires. This nightmare could be nothing or it could be everything. I would say write down everything you remember of this nightmare and maybe talk to the psychiatrist that releases you," he said to James.

"Okay. I will do that," he responded back. He has no intention of doing so. "Maybe it was just nothing but a nightmare because I feel trapped her on the ward. Anyway, thanks for the info doc."

"Is there anything else? I was told by the nursing staff that you're getting very close one of our regular patients."

"You mean Angel," James said.

"I do, that is something of interest if you'd like to discuss. I know Angel well, and while we can't talk about her condition or even about her, we can talk about you," he said.

James felt uncomfortable at the direction that the conversation was now going, and it was unexpected. He didn't know that the nurses keep track of all their activity. That was the only way that the doctor would know who he is hanging with regularly.

"She is helping me with some stuff. No big."

"And Ryan?" he asked.

"I think we get that continuing to feud will get us nowhere. Besides people like Ryan are just looking for attention and I just want out of here. You won't be hearing about anymore tussles from the two of us," James said.

"Then that will conclude our session. Just to let you know your next meeting will not be with me on Tuesday. I'm the temporary doctor only here for the holidays. Your regularly scheduled psychiatrist will be the main ward doctor," he said.

"Okay, that is good to know, thanks again, doc."

With that James left the office. He made his way through the dining area but when he reached the nursing station he was stopped by a nurse.

"James. It is almost visiting hours. Do you want visitors today? Your family and girlfriend both called to see if you were taking visitors."

"Sure, can you contact them and tell them that I will see them today?"

"Of course, James," the nurse said back.

James made his way back to his room. He knew it was the one place that Angel could not go to find him. He had decided that right then he had to figure out what was up and what was down without her. He wanted to know why the dream was so much a part of the present. The hold that the darkness now had upon him. It was all too much, and Angel only made things more clouded.

What James wanted more than anything was to be centered again. Maybe if he could dissect the dream maybe it would leave his mind. Here is what he knew.

The darkness was not ominous he knew that, it has kept him from rushing to the end where he was laying covered in blood. Was the darkness then telling him something? *Okay that was a good start,* James thought.

It meant that the darkness in the dream and the darkness that he felt inside his very soul right now was different. The darkness in the dream was his friend, maybe even his subconscious helping him through the worst parts of his decisions of late.

The blood was clearly his and it was on the floor because he was bleeding during the dream from his wrists. The smell was of wet metal was blood, was something that he had smelt before when he was with Angel in the atrium. That is why it was so familiar. It was blood nothing else. At least not yet.

It was time to think about the first door. The scene of James lying in the hospital bed and the most glaring was Victoria, pregnant and married to James and yet he still hurt her in the end. His family all around him, and he had hurt them just like now. That was a possible reality and his mind was telling him that the paths that he was now on and it could end this way. The darkness was showing him that no matter what if he was never willing to change, it would hurt the ones James loved. He would hurt Victoria and their future. Change. That was the key here and it was something he needed to hold on to truly understand what this dream meant.

Moving himself through the dream he remembered how the darkness had moved him in the dream to the next place. It was James but he was even less of himself. He was alone and while he looked alive it was clear that this version of himself was the result of losing everyone that he loved. That James badly need hygiene and a bath. This James was still cutting away at his skin and that bothered him now that he was reflecting. Was this the darkness trying to tell him what would happen if he loses everything if he could not come to terms with his mental illness? It was not the worst thing he could imagine. He could even live like this version of himself. It meant he was still alive even if it was as a zombie that never showered. It was better than some realities in this dream.

He was dreading this next part and thought he thought he might skip it, no need to see himself happy in a reality that would never be true. But he promised himself that he would go through everything and analyze it.

This part of the dream was Victoria and James in happier times. In the beginning of their relationship they had always talked about where they would go with their relationship, a real future. She would finish school, she was going to be a lawyer, and they would move to New York City. James would write, like he always wanted to, and they would be happy raising a family in the city. They were both small town California kids and it would be the perfect life.

James figured that was why the darkness has shown him this vision of his future. One of happiness that he would never know. Victoria would soon find out, he made the decision to tell her about Angel, and she would leave him. As strong as their love was it could not stand this test. James decided that the darkness was just showing him a reality — true or not it mattered less. Happiness was not in the cards for James.

James was no longer in this room but back in the
corridor in the dream. The streaks of wet metallic smelling
blood were still fresh in his mind. This was the most
important thing that the darkness had shown James. His
future. Death by bleeding out from cut up wrists. Twice he
had seen this but the last was so vivid. He was alone, so
alone. No one else cared about this James. He had clearly
lost everyone, and it was not pretty. He was in the dream
again, more than ever since he began to dissect the dream.
His dying self was crying out, but why? If it was over why
was he trying to get James to save himself? It was the
biggest puzzle of all. This James had clearly called out in
hopes that the James walking through the dream would
hear and see. The darkness was showing that this was his
future—James was sure of that.

"James, your girlfriend is here to see you," a nurse said
peeking through his opened door. He had lost track of time
while inside his mind and thoughts.

"Okay," he said quickly getting up from his bed. As he
walked towards the dining area where visitors met with
patients, he knew the conversation with Victoria was going
to be the worst he would ever have in his life. Out of the
corner of his eye he saw Angel sitting on a couch watching
television. He walked past her, not wanting to meet her
eyes.

Victoria was there as she always was, smiling at James
lighting up his world. In that moment he could see the
vision of Victoria and him dancing away happy as can be in
their New York City apartment. That smile made him feel
like the guiltiest man in the world.

When she came in for an embrace and a kiss, he turned
letting her kiss his cheek. Victoria was taken aback by this
and she frowned for the first time.

"Is everything okay," she said sitting down.

"We need to talk—"

"Wow. No conversation that starts that way is ever good. What's going on James are you okay?" she asked.

"I'm fine, look Vic, you know I love you, but do you really think that you can handle what is to come in the days, weeks, and months maybe even the years from now? I'm not going to get better overnight and I'm in for some of the darkest days I have ever lived through," he said.

"I will always be here for the long run. You know that James. Don't tell me that you're starting to doubt us."

James was not doubting them as a couple. He was just doubting himself, "I love you—"

"You keep saying that and it's scaring me. What is it?" she asked in earnest.

"There is someone here that has been helping me. Her name is Angel."

"Helping you how?" she asked.

"Just helping. It has been in hell in here and I'm dealing with a lot with the stuff that got me here," he responded.

Victoria took his hands into hers. "Look James, I'm not an idiot I know things are tough in here and there is not much I can do. I love you and if this girl is helping you—"

"I kissed her."

With a single motion her hands were out of his, and he could see the hurt in her eyes. A single tear began to fall down her cheek but wiped it away quickly.

"Do you love her?"

"No. I love you, Victoria."

"Obviously not," she said quickly.

Before James could say another word, she got up from the table and left through the exit. James wanted so bad to go after her, but he had hurt her more than she was letting on. James was in pieces. It was not supposed to go that way, and yet it went exactly how it was supposed to be. He figured Victoria would never talk to him again.

He wanted nothing more to be alone and he again walked past Angel without looking to see if she was still there on the couch. The darkness had a hold of him, but nothing mattered. He had lost Victoria for good and there was no going back. He found his room empty not just of his roommate but his things. James figured that he had requested another room. He was okay with being alone. It would most likely be that way for the rest of his life.

Part Thirteen

IT WAS PITCH BLACK. Someone was sitting on his bed. It was a long moment before dream and reality came rushing into his view. He was back in the dream, but now he was no longer there, instead she was sitting there staring at him.

"You avoided me all day," she said to the silence.

"It was a bad day all around. I had the worst nightmare in my life and, well, you saw what happened in the dining hall with my girlfriend," he said back.

"I did. Sorry, I have a feeling that you told her the truth, I would have advised against that if you had asked me," she said back.

"It had to be done," he said. He looked around in the darkness. "How in the hell did you get past the nurses to my room."

She laughed as if it was obvious, "I know this place better than anyone. I know how the nurses work and when they're doing their rounds. I often spend my time here. I like to watch you sleep."

This was a surprise to James and one he had not expected. "What do you mean you spend most nights here?"

"I was here last night. You were having a horrible dream. I thought about waking you up, but I know a night terror dream when I see one. You don't wake people from those," she said.

"So, you just watched me. How did you avoid my roommate? How did I miss you when I got up?"

"I'm a small person, you or your roommate never saw me," she said. Angel laid down next to James on the bed and reactively he put his arms around her. Their faces were inches apart.

"You hurt me today. I wanted to see you all day and you avoided me," she said. She put her hands-on James face. "I'm glad you told your girlfriend the truth now we can get closer."

With that Angel began to kiss James passionately and it was so easy for him to give in. His hands roamed all across her body and she made small moans of appreciation. James began to undress her, and Angel allowed him to first to remove the thin white tank top made it easy to reveal her small but beautiful breasts.

Angel removed her bottoms and even in the darkness James knew she was shaven. She removed his pajama pants revealing that he was ready for her. He reached down and felt her. With one motion he was inside of her and she bit down on his shoulder to keep from screaming. He continued to go in and out of her, working her up into frenzy. He slowed letting her recover. He turned her over letting her lay on her back. He looked into her eyes and saw only passion. He entered her again and it was pure pleasure for both, and for a while they became one.

It was a long while as they lay together entangled in the dark and the silence was that of two people who had become closer than ever. In a single day James had lost Victoria but gained Angel. She was a small thing next to him, James had never noticed this. Angel was looking up at him waiting to see what he would say. He wasn't sure. It was amazing being with her, but he felt different—he felt guilty. Had things really been over with Victoria? He didn't know, but they would be changed forever.

"That was amazing," he said. Angel smiled at this. She got up putting her clothes back on in the dark.

"Do you have to leave? I wouldn't mind another go," he said.

"I have to go before the nurses come around for their nightly checks," she said. Fully dressed again she bent down and kissed James. "Maybe we can do this again. You're mine now, you know that, right?"

With that she disappeared out the door, and James knew she was right.

Part Fourteen

MORNING CAME, AND JAMES was more confused than ever. His night of passion with Angel was amazing and she was the only girl other than Victoria that he had ever been with in that way. With Victoria it was always as if they were one and the love was bonding them when they had sex. With Angel it had been more animalistic passion that was driving him. He could not say which one he preferred better. He would leave that question for another day.

James was feeling better as he made his way to breakfast, and he realized that he had made it to Tuesday. It was a week since he had made the decision to take his life. To his surprise Angel was not there like he had hoped. He ate his breakfast halfheartedly and his eyes could not help but look around for Angel. When breakfast concluded James made his way to nurses' station in hopes of to ask the whereabouts of Angel.

The nurses knew right away why he was there, "I'm sorry, James. Angel is not going to be here until later today. She is being punished. She was out wondering the halls last and she is in the isolation room. She put up quite a fight with the staff. She will be out later this afternoon."

James felt a tinge of guilt, but he didn't ask Angel to come to his room. In some ways it was good that all they thought was that she was running around late at night. He had survived his time in the isolation room, but when he thought about it for a moment Angel was different. Could she survive time alone?

"Just make sure you check on her, we don't want her going down the wrong path again. Please, tell her that I will be here when she gets out."

"I can do that, James."

James made his way to his room to find a good book to read for the day. It was going to be a slow one for James.

It was late afternoon when his mother came to visit. She had not been back since Friday, and he was glad to see someone other than the loves of his life. The visit was a welcoming one. They talked about the possibility of James going home the next day. He told her to be optimistic but there was no guarantee that he would for sure get out the next day.

"I will have to talk to the doctor first and he will get the final say," he said.

"Have you been doing better?"

"Yes, mom," he said with an eye roll.

"I just want you home, son," she said.

"I know."

It was at moment that he finally saw Angel for the first time that day. She looked like she had been through a lot and she didn't look up initially at James until she passed him. His mother didn't notice the exchange, but the look on her face was different. He had seen that look the last time they found her in her room with cuts on her. It was look of defeat. James did not like this, and the rest of his visit with his mother was long and his mind was not on his mother.

He didn't get a chance to see her during dinner or the movie night. When he was sure she was not going to show up he retired to his room. While there he was lost in his thoughts about how Angel had looked.

James was already asleep when Angel made her way to his room. He was happy to see her, not because he thought he would get lucky, but because he was genuinely worried about her.

"Are you okay?" he asked to the darkness. He knew she was there, but she was silent. He sat up taking her face into his hands. Her eyes were blank as if she didn't know where she was at in this moment. "What happened to you in there?"

With that, Angel looked at James for the first time. It was like she was possessed by something, and James knew right away what it was going on. The darkness had taken her over.

Angel finally talked to a relieved James, "I can't do this anymore."

"You mean us?"

"No," she said. She brought her hands to his face, "I'm saying that I can't do this life anymore. I can't do this, James. I have to end it. I can't let this continue. I can't let the darkness win."

"What about last night? You were so happy. We were so happy together."

"I was happy to be with you. I wanted to end my life when I came by last night to tell you, but what happened only delayed those feelings. It was amazing what happened, but it changes nothing."

She started to get off the bed, but James stopped her gently grabbing her arm, "Don't do this. We can be happy together. We'll get out of here and we will start a life together. Leave all this behind and never look back."

She sat down again and for a moment there was glimmer of hope, but the despair returned on her face. "We can be together, forever. Let's do it. End our lives together."

It hit James as if he knew all along. The nightmare. The darkness leading him down to the end of the corridor. Yesterday he thought it was something good. Trying to show him that the path he was going could end in so many ways. He recognized the darkness because it was familiar— it was Angel the darkness embodiment. He knew it, and everything was leading to this moment. She was pushing him. He was at a crossroads. Angel wanted his life, it was the only way they could be together. He knew what he had to do.

"I can't do it, Angel. I love you and I think you should think about that and not do this, please. We can have a good life. I can give you a good life."

She smiled a smile that was both manic and dangerous. "You said we could be together forever. The only way we can end the darkness is by ending our lives. I told you, you're mind. I'm yours. You have to do this with me, James."

"No, I chose to live with you, not without you. Why can't we be together and alive?" he said in anger. In that moment he could feel it leaving his soul. It would always be there, but it was faint, almost non-existent now—he had chosen for the first time since coming to the ward—he wanted to really live a life outside this place.

"Please. Live. Survive. You will get out of here and we will end your darkness together. Please, Angel."

"Fine. You live, James. I will do what I have to."

Angel got up faster than James could anticipate, and she was out of his room in a flash. He struggled to get up lost in the entanglement of his blankets but determining to run after her. When he got outside his door, he was met quickly by a nurse, but Angel was nowhere to be found.

"What are you doing out of your room so late at night, James?" she asked. She stopped his momentum. *Where the hell was Angel and how did this nurse not see her.*

"I saw Angel," he said. He thought about what he was going to say. She had been in his room and she had told him that she was going to kill herself? He chose to tell the truth.

"Look. Angel was just in my room she was trying to tell me that she wanted to end her life. She literally just ran past you," he said quickly.

"Angel didn't pass me young man. What are you trying to pull—"

James was not in the mood for this and he ducked running past the nurse.

"Mel, I need help," the nurse yelled to his back. From the nurse's station stepped out a very tall and muscular nurse who caught James knocking the wind out of him trying to contain him.

"Where are you going, James? It's too late in the night for shenanigans," he said.

It took him several breathes before he started again, "Angel was in my room and she said that she is going to kill herself. You have to stop her. She had to have run past you. Did you not see her?"

The nurse Mel looked at James funny, "No one has run pass me and Angel is in her room right now."

"You're not listening," James tried to shake Nurse Mel to no avail, "Please!"

By then the female nurse had caught up to the pair, she was panting. "I tried to tell him that no one but him ran pass me."

"YOU'RE NOT LISTENING!"

"Okay, James," nurse Mel said. "Go and check Angel's room. It will give us all peace of mind."

With an exasperated look at both Nurse Mel and James she made her way down to the girl's dormitory. The scream that came from the nurse was all James needed to know.

Part Fifteen

JAMES WAS SITTING in the office of Dr. Mary Seager, his therapist for the last three years of his life. It was a long ride to get here, but he was ready to finally talk about that night.

"You said that you finally ready to talk about it, James. What happened that night? What was real and what was fake."

"I'm ready."

"What do you remember?"

This was an interesting question. The night she was asking was one that he vowed never to talk about because he didn't know what was real and what was not. It was only through therapy that he was here and trying to find reasoning in that night.

"I thought Angel had come to my room. We had a conversation about leaving that place, but she wanted to end her life along with me by her side. She wanted us to end it together."

"But that was not real, was it?"

"No. It was something my mind dreamed up. It seemed all too real at the time."

"Often our minds can take us to places we never thought, but it's not always real," she said.

"It might not have been real, but what happened really did happen and it was all my fault. At least I felt like it was for so long. Now I know there was nothing I could have done."

"It sounds like survivor's guilt. James, you know the whole story. You have for three years. Angel had been dead for hours before you dreamed that she was in your room. There was nothing you could have done. She made the decision to leave this world without you. It was tragic and you felt something for her, but she's gone. Can you let her go now?" she asked.

"I know that she was dead, Dr. Seager, but I don't get why I dreamt that she came to me. I could let it go if I could understand why the dream felt real. I touched her skin."

"Dreams are an interesting thing. Some doctors try and analyze them and find some meaning. You told me over the course of the last year the nightmare that you had. That it was Angel that was the darkness. It was leading to your death and hers. Yet, it was only her death in the end. Perhaps there's something to this train of thought. Angel was your way of finding yourself. In the last three years you have moved to New York, got married to Victoria, and in my professional opinion, got your life back together."

"It's all true, but today is the three-year anniversary. All I could think about was what if I could have known."

"You have experience with suicide and now loss alongside survivor's guilt. What you're feeling is what your own family went thought when they saw you laying in that hospital bed. What could they have done different? It's all relative because if you wanted to die, they would have trouble stopping you. I'm not advocating suicide, far from it. But build on your experience. You wanted to live but at one point you wanted to end your life. I know you feel guilty. You cared about Angel, but she made her own decision to take her life just like you did once."

James knew she was right. That night was the worst and best thing to happen in his life. When the doctors told James the next day that Angel had been gone for hours and there was no way she was in his room he didn't believe at the time. She was so real. The way she touched his face. The look that she gave him. The conversation about ending their lives together. But it was all a dream. He woke in a panic and the rest was out of his control.

After that day when he lost Angel, he decided living was a much better way to spend his life. He left the ward two days later and fixed his life. Somehow Victoria found a way to forgive him after he thought that she was lost to him forever, and they were happy. He promised to seek help and two weeks later they moved to New York. James found Dr. Seager and got to a point in his life where he moved on. Victoria was now towards the end of her law degree.

The day that James asked her to marry him was on a trip Paris, and though it was cliché, he proposed on the Eiffel Tower. Somehow Angel had given him his life back, and though he missed her he was in the life he was supposed to be living.

"Tomorrow is a big day for you, isn't it?"

"It's a very important day. My book will be officially released."

"What was it called again," she asked.

"Angel on the Ward."

Author Bio

James Edgar Skye is a native of Salinas, California, and goes by the moniker "The Bipolar Writer." James was first diagnosed with Bipolar One in 2007. He has since added panic disorder and social anxiety, but he is no longer defined by these identities. Since 2017, he has been a mental health advocate creating the blog "The Bipolar Writer Collaborative Blog." In this place, he shares his mental illness experiences alongside other writers with mental illnesses. In March of 2020, James self-published his first literary work, *The Bipolar Writer: A Memoir*. In the same year, James began life coaching to learn the detach, stay in the moment, opening up to his feelings that he kept hidden, and finished in December. James has been working on his inner I and trusting the process has allowed James to grow as a human being and a writer. He began The Bipolar Writer Podcast in late 2020, which will continue his mental health advocacy work, and he is considering starting a non-profit in 2021.

James is working on a Master of Fine Arts in Creative Writing and English with completion in early 2021. He holds a Bachelor of Fine Arts in Creative Writing and English from Southern New Hampshire University, where he graduated summa cum laude.

Writing is a significant part of J.E.'s life, and he writes nonfiction, fantasy fiction, novellas, poetry, and screenplays. In 2021, James will launch his LLC ghostwriting business, "The Bipolar Writer Ghostwriting Services." When he isn't writing, he enjoys role-playing video games, reading a spectrum of literature, and watching his favorite sports teams. James has a love for Japanese or Korean food and music.

http://www.jamesedgarskye.me
http://www.thebipolarwriter.blog
https://www.patreon.com/jamesedgarskye
http://www.twitter.com/JamesEdgarSkye
http://www.facebook.com/JamesedgarSkye

Made in the USA
Monee, IL
17 December 2020

53692405R00075